Crossed Oars

I0587639

Kate Deller-Evans

Crossed Oars

Acknowledgements

This story began as a Negotiated Project in the Advanced Diploma of Arts (Professional Writing) at the Adelaide College of the Arts and I would like to thank my various teachers there.

Parts of this novel were read on Radio Adelaide by Cath Keneally.

Crossed Oars
ISBN 978 1 74027 925 3
Copyright © text Kate Deller-Evans 2015
Cover photos: Marina Deller-Evans

First published 2015 by
GINNINDERRA PRESS
PO Box 3461 Port Adelaide SA 5015
www.ginninderrapress.com.au

Contents

For my brother John and my daughter Rosie, rowers both

December

In the inter-school triathlon

I don't wait to brake the wheels
but throw my leg over the bar,
fling the bike out from under,
where it clatters to the rope
and I hit the bitumen in a run
counting only four girls ahead.

On the corner of Esplanade and Semaphore Road
the traffic lights turn red
and I tell my brain, *No, keep going!*
Go Lighthouse, go iron girl!
Want to score the bloody points
for the team
– whatever.

The water's edge looms,
choked as I might feel
if I wasn't actually enjoying this,
and I splash in behind the others,
more coming up behind me too.

The whole school aquatics club
in the area competition
and I'm not doing too bad,
I think, for a Year 9,
sure, nearly Year 10,
and the water's a slap of cold
as I throw my body in
and swim.

Swim.

The end of the jetty close now,
I only have to loop
the last pylon
then make it back to shore.

Panting, wet, bronze-medal place,
youngest on the podium.
Even if I only get a ribbon
and we stand beneath the shelter
with barely any spectators,
I feel like I've achieved
some – not insignificant –
thing.

I face Bailey

after school, back down the jetty
leaning over the rails
and complain, 'You didn't see me race!'

'Yeah, well. Knew you'd do good, kid.'
Bailey bumps hips with me.
'But I'm not really into
all that swimming stuff.'

'Besides,' she says,
'that team mentality thing.'

I feel a sulk coming on,
then rally, pathetically quick.
'At least we live by the sea!'

Looking down, the line of seaweed
shadows aqua-green –
it's a long walk out
before deep water
– sand's taken over,
drifting in from the south.

Bailey says, her words a monotone,
'Christmas hols soon.'

I don't think she's as bored
as she sounds. Maybe restless.

'Whatcha gonna do?'
She bumps me again.

I look out across the gulf,
not actual ocean waters,
but I figure it counts.

'Sail across the seven seas!'
I silly-sing, in pantomime.

'Yeah, right,' she says.
'Come on. Let's get an ice cream.'

She turns to walk back
but stops me first
stares hard.
'What we really need
is proper boyfriends.'

What, I think, *not just
blind drunk groping in the dark?*

I skip back
along the jetty,
bellowing,
'All you need is love.'

'Ant an' Fish'll do,'
she calls after me.

Bending double,
I croak the rest of it,
'Love. Love is all you need.'
Then I pretend gag.

'Honestly, TC,
you should grow up.'

Then Bailey sprints off
across to Semaphore Road
and the Icecreamery.

Bailey lives

a few streets back in a cottage in an alley
whereas I live right on the Esplanade,
not a fancy house, just plain wood
– round here lots are weather-worn
despite New Port developments on the rise.

Mum and me, and Sammy.
Bailey's mum has a new baby too
but Bailey hates its father,
who makes her mum keep boxed nappies
in her room with a change table.
Now, the only bit of space
Bailey can claim as her own
stinks.

At least Sammy's nearly a toddler
so after dinner most nights Mum and me
wheel his pusher down the jetty
to the shaded playground.

When I was young, there was an old swing set.
I used to aim high and remember watching
people heading out
loaded with bags and rods.

Best of all I loved looking at the angel
on top of the war memorial
guarding over us below.

Sammy's father

is a mystery
Mum won't discuss

just as much as

she won't discuss mine.

So I don't ask any more.

When I enter our place round the side
I'm surprised to find Mum

not in her potting shed or at the kiln

but waiting for me

rocking on the back porch rocking chair.

Papers in Mum's lap

look like a pile of letters –
one printed and official
the other handwritten –
but I can't make out
who they're from.

She's rocking fit to bust
so I perch on the grey wooden bench,
pull a leftover lunch apple
out of my backpack
and munch.

'I went for a job.'
She says the words
in time with her rocking.

'Hey! Great one!
What sort?'

'I can't make enough money
just selling stuff, you know.'

'I s'pose,' I say,
having watched her for years
coiling snakes of clay,
smoothing them into bowls,
pinching little faces in,
firing them hard.

'It's this house,' she explains.
'I know I got it cheap, as far as prices go,
but with the credit squeeze…'

It's an unusual speech for Mum,
who never talks money,
bills or difficulties.
I'm not used to her whingeing
so I chew the apple,
focus on the back wall,
the garden's straggly palm trees,
a spiny-thorned pomegranate bush
and two seagulls, squabbling.

'Tabitha Caitlin!
Are you listening to me?'

I examine the apple.
I'm nearly to its core.

'And what with the price of living,
how exactly are we going to cope?'
Her voice goes up with the question.

'But you'll get the job, Mum.'

'That's what I'm afraid of.'

With a jolt I realise
there's fear mixed with anger
in her reply.

She jumps from the chair

and runs inside
to little Sammy crying,
awake from his nap,

leaving the wicker chair
rocking on its own.

I lob the last of my apple
at the seagulls.

Got 'em.

In the last week of school

teachers practically give up.
'If you come to school,' Mr Aird said,
'you'll just be helping me stack tables.'

Mum's retort was predictable.
'You're going, whether they like it or not,'
so I'm here stacking tables
when I suddenly see her, my own mother,
in the corridor with the principal,
bitch-face gorgon Brody.

Don't get me wrong, I don't really
waste my time hating her too much
but it makes me dark she thinks so little of me,
poking fun at my long blonde hair –
its streaks are natural,
I can't help looking like I do.
I'm no idiot or anything
but she treats me like I am.

Mum's talking and Brody's nodding.
As they walk past my room the gorgon looks in,
sees me and smiles, a tight little number,
and I feel I've turned to stone.

Mum's head is bowed and I don't even think
she knows I'm here,
fixed, watching her as she walks by.

So?

I demand when I get back home.
Mum's spooning banana mashed in yoghurt
into Sammy's mouth,
concentrating on the task.

'He should be feeding himself now,'
I tell her off, put on my own
mother-knows-best voice.

'I got the job. It starts next year.'
She doesn't look at me
when she speaks.
Instead, makes baby faces
at my brother.

There's some catch, I can feel it.
I say it slow, 'And…
the problem is…'

She puts down the spoon and turns.
'We have to move. The job's across town.
It's a residential,
in the foothills.'

'It's a what?'

my voice cracks
almost to a screech.

'We're going to live in,' she tells me,
'rent our own house out to tenants,
move to the good school's place
specially for its art teacher, off-campus.

'It will mean our financial salvation,'
she says.

But I can't believe a school
has its own special staff house.

'I'm not going,' I say.
'Flat out. No.'

'It's all arranged.' Her voice is chirpy.
'Tomorrow we go visit your new school.
Book you in.'

Tears prickle my lids,
my cheeks flush hot.
'I'm not going. Not to some
stuck-up private bloody college.'

'Course not, sweetheart.' She gives me that
oh-I'm-sorry-you-don't-get-it look.
'We couldn't even afford
the reduced fees.
No, your school's a short train ride
further up the hill from my school.'

The hill? Hills? What is that?
The beach is all I've known.
Here, this house, this home, my friends, my school,
the water, jetty, waves.

'Come on, my little Tabby Cat,' croons Mum.
She reaches out to take my chin,
turns my face to hers.

Sun through the window behind
haloes her red frizz,
smudged liner round her eyes.

'Say something,' she begs.

But even my silly-singing voice
has fled.

At Acacia High

Principal Carrick looks like an extra
from Hogwarts, or Miss Cackle's Academy,
a witch, but not quite bitch-face Brody.

With her hair swept into a tight bun
and her eyebrows pencilled on,
she has a voice that's commanding
and when she reads my end-of-year report
I squirm.

'Well, at least you excel in sport,'
she sighs. 'But we don't have swimming
here at Acacia High, Tabitha.
Only the Year 8s have their carnival.
And you've missed that, dear, haven't you?'

She peers over half-rim glasses
and eyeballs me, as if it's my fault
I'm coming in at this stage,
didn't begin at the start of high.

'There's only one thing for it.
You'll have to go into rowing.
As a Year 10, new recruit,
you'll probably manage.
Otherwise, no harm done,
you can pull out.'
She signs some paperwork, turns to Mum.

'You're lucky to get her in.
Places are hard to get.
This is the best public school
in the state, you know.
I expect your daughter to appreciate that
and do well.'

She looks at me speculatively.
'Ah, as well as she can do.'

And she puts her head back down.

Mum gives me that wide-eyed look that says,
'I think we've been dismissed. Come on,
let's make tracks while we can.'
And while Ms Carrick
appears busy with more pressing writing,
acting as if we're already gone,
we scuff backwards out the door.

After two weeks, my room

looks like an emptied conch.
All the junk I've had to toss,
collections to abandon.

Bailey's helped.
She divided up the baby toys
– some for her little sister
– some for Sammy.

I can't believe I'd kept them
such a long time.

Barbie Ken hurls through the air
and smacks me on the arm.

'Hey! Give me a break!'

I clutch him to my chest,
mock a kiss to his crown.

'He's been a Prince Charming
to all my beauties, you know.'

'Yeah, right. Ya mean
these poor creatures?
Half are headless, TC.
The rest have crap haircuts!'
She lifts them in a fan.
'Were you trying out
for an apprenticeship?'

I snatch away the poor Barbies.

'Scrap them, then,' I say.
'They're no use to anyone.'

My toys are divided into three piles

For Bailey's sister:
the silver rattle from our neighbour, Mrs Dyson –
Baby Cheri can gummie it with her dribble.
The plushies, Baby Born that drinks and wets, and the
fur-trimmed telephone – all to cuddle, change and
gossip into when she's older.
Like I did.

For Sammy:
squashy pillow horse – he can ride,
then fall asleep on.
The bath-time boats – I floated them
through my childhood:
red-sailed yacht, blue barge
and the yellow speedboat,
all set for a quick getaway.

Stuff that goes into the shed:
the plastic box of Lego – those palaces I built,
towns dreamt up, and beachside resorts.
The half-constructed galleon,
cannons and sailor captain.
A parrot for the pirate's shoulder,
the dinghy and the dungeon,
haunted by the ghost.
A box that we can open again –
When?

Later, in my dreams

I'm a seagull.
Dusk is falling,
we must fly to the north,
fly low, over sand dunes.

Below, a child points up,
calls out.

I hear a pop,

have a pain
under my wing,

have been shot,
and plummet
down into the water,

other seagulls
tweeting away.

I can feel me
drowning,
my wings useless,

dark water
closing over.

Sammy is crying when I wake

and I'm soaked in sweat
from the dream
and heat
– bet he's wet too.

Then Mum calls out
for me to get him up
out of his cot
and dressed
since she's opening the door
to the removalists
ready to cart our stuff away.

Last night we ate the last
leftovers of Christmas food –
for brekky today
Mum's promised Maccas
on the way.

I jackknife off the mattress
(all that remains in my room),
haul Sammy from his blankie,
struggle with his jammies
– half-soaked, as I thought.

Our neighbour Mrs Dyson hallos her way in,
rescues me
from the gro-suit and Huggies tussle
to calm my pounding heart
with the tea she's brought in
– mine sugary.

We are leaving, we are leaving
thunders in my temples.
All that I have known
I will lose.
All who are known to me
will be gone.
Everything familiar
vanish.

But to go
across the town
the blocks and roads and gardens
halfway to the moon?

Mr Dyson is directing the men,
singlets and trackie-daks,
tattoos and loud voices.
One winks at me
and I clam up,
pick up Sammy out of the way
and walk across the garden
out to the street and into the car.

'Come see us any time,'
calls Mrs Dyson from the footpath.

Mum's got the windows wound down
and yells back,
'Look after the tenants, Dorothy.
They're nice people, I think.'

'I'll miss you all!'
Her voice floats in
and our car leaves the kerb
drifts into Esplanade traffic

with the sights and sounds
of Semaphore
melting
away.

At a table in Glenelg Maccas

I feed Sammy
half my final hotcake
dripping in buttery syrup
and Mum hands me a tiny present.

'But I've already got my Chrissie gift.'
I pat the slender mobile
tucked tight in my jeans pocket.

This is a puzzle and a treat.
A locket in a satin box,
two mini photos,
Sammy and Mum.

'We're the constants in your life, love,'
she says. 'You can count on us
whatever is to come.'

I feel like my heart's dropped
into my belly
and the food is leaden,
a lump stuck in my gullet.

'Remember what Ms Carrick said?
They'd got a new girl from the country too
so you won't be the only fresh face at school.'

I laugh to think of my face as fresh.
'And we've enrolled you
so you're in time for that camp.'

She's trying to cheer me along,
has guessed how scared I am.

I don't want to go, to move,
have any change at all.

The rowing camp goes for a week,
the one before the term begins
no time at all away from now.

Wish I could just stay
curled up tight at home,
the one we've left,
on and on and on,
no change at all.

Outside

by the strip of fast food shops
the tram terminates near a memorial,
a model of the tall ship
that brought settlers to the state.

As Mum puts Sammy in the pusher
I watch a good-looking girl
about my own age
cross the roundabout
bee-lining for the tram.
With her is a tall guy,
dark hair, pink cheeks, pale eyes,
I note as he walks by.

The girl is punching his arm
talking ten-to-the-dozen.
He is warding her off,
lifting his hands above his head
but laughing, happy.

My heart does a funny flip-flop.
All others around him blur
and I see only him.
Then Sammy's buckled in
and we have to be off.

I turn to strain for a last look
but the pair have boarded the tram,
its glass windows opaque.

In the new place

as soon as the boxes are unpacked
my phone goes off
and I read Bailey's text.

Hi tc
Thinking of you
Xxbails
Write back
Xx
Im bored

Bored! If only.
I write back:
Im ok
In new house.
Its not quiet
here though.
We are on the
train tracks!

Bailey return texts
as soon as I've sent it.
Wanna c
flix?
Sema4 show.

I punch out an answer
in return, *Sure*
will see if i can

Mum's staring at the kitchen
cupboards that were built
before the Ark
and the house
smells stale
and abandoned.

So much for posh.

'Sure,' she says
to my request.
'You can take the train
from here to town
then back down
to Semaphore.'

As a long freight train rattles by
I can barely hear her tell me,
'The station's right next door.'

Der.

I text Bailey when I'm near Glanville

the stop closest to the beach,
though it's a bit of a hike from there
since they lifted the rails
up from the centre of Semaphore Road.

Mrs Dyson once told me
how it used to bring city folk
down for a seaside break.
Ferris wheels and sideshows
all dismantled now.

Bailey texts
Ant & fish
Wanna come 2
Ok?

When I step off the train
they're all there.
Fish standing aside on his own,
Bailey and Ant too close.

Bailey's face is all blotchy
and she speaks in a rush
as we set off down the road.

The telltale sign is when
Ant reaches out to hold her hand.
These guys who've been our mates
but no way boyfriend material.

Fish walks so close to me
and I push away memories
of nights with him
Bailey doesn't know about
and I don't want to remember.

Now it's like I haven't got wing-room
even seagulls give each other
and I'm seriously creeped out.

When the movie's done

the happy couple want to head
to the Icecreamery, but I say no.
They snogged so much
I doubt they saw any of the show
and Fish's making such fish lips at me
I want to slip out of his reach,
stand far, far away.

Bailey's annoyed.
'It wouldn't hurt, you know,'
she whispers.
'Then we could be a real gang again.'

But I think we're both relieved
when the train finally comes
and she can go back for an ice cream.

And more suck face.

January

Shelley, one of the coaches

phones, confirming my commitment
to the rowing camp.

'No need for previous experience,' she says.
'You'll really enjoy it.
All you gotta do is train hard.'

She flings out the comment
as if it's easy, nothing.
And the heavy physical training
she refers to
is something everyone can do.

I think with longing of my swim team.
We weren't that serious. Just a bit of fun.
Something good to do

if you live by the beach.
But rowing? I've never set foot in a boat,
not even a dinghy. Oh, taken a ride
on the *Popeye* once. Does that count?

I feel as if I'm in free-fall.
The idea of something
so left of field is weird.
I'm like a boat myself
let off its moorings.

I could be anyone or do anything.
Who's to say if I can or can't row?

No one who knows me now
will ever know.

Bailey might say, *Why try?*
I could answer, *Why not?*

'The skills are simple,' Shelley adds.
'And you'll get to travel.'

Mum has listened in to the call.
'It'll be good for you to go, sweetheart.
You've been hanging round too much
and I've a term of lessons to prepare.'

From his ride-on car,
she lifts Sammy into the air,
spins him round.

'You, young sir, must likewise
prepare thyself for childcare!'

His bottom lip quivers, though
I doubt he knows what she's on about,
then I think,
We're all of us
stepping out
into uncharted waters.

Walker Flat

on the River Murray
where the banks are brown, the river's brown
and the only green is from the willows
when there's a bit of a bend.

Mum and Sammy drop me off to a camp
as busy as the sunset fair at Semaphore
except everyone here's in rowing shorts and singlets.
So many guys, so many babes
looking focused, purposeful.

I'm allocated a bunk,
thrown into a provisional crew.
New rowers and junior rowers
are given a pep talk by coaches.

'My name's Joseph, Joe to you,
and I'm here to tell you
rowing's a safe sport.'

The speaker, with black curly hair,
lovely olive skin, smiles a wide smile.

'But there are hazards.'

'Like what?' asks a gangly girl
towering beside me.

'In the Murray there're snags – you know,
submerged logs and branches
that can catch you unawares.'

I nearly silly-sing out loud
When you go down to the woods today
but clamp my mouth shut
thankfully, and have only the idiot voice
singing silently in my head.

Beside me, the tall one pipes up again,
'And water snakes?'

'Sure, and the water itself's dangerous,'
adds the female coach,
who I realise must be Shelley.

Joe wags a finger at us.
'You need to be fit, and confident swimmers.'

From my side I hear an intake of breath.

'And know safety regulations.'

'You'll get used to training hard.
Rowing will make you tough.'

'And tough-minded.'

A snigger from the back alerts me
most of these rowers have heard it all before.
I can't be the only newbie, though
the girl beside me looks as nervous as I feel
and as ignorant as I clearly am.

At breakfast

me and the tall girl
are taken under the wings of two others.
Sarah and Alex, they tell us.
Together we make up a scratch crew.

I try to gauge the lie of the land,
what to anticipate on the river.

Alex makes me feel like a sparrow
in the company of an eagle.
Stocky and well-muscled,
she exudes such confidence.
Right now, her focus rests
squarely on the food.

Sarah digs me in the ribs.

'Don't worry about her,'
she stage whispers.
'Outside of a boat she's silent enough
but on the water she's as explosive
as a fireworks display.'

Sarah continues to chatter.
She knows a lot about rowing,
says it runs in her veins.
There's something familiar about her,
I have no idea what.
We can't have met before.
Acacia kids live in the hills
south-east of the city.
I've only ever been north-west
at the beach.

The tall one is too busy eating to talk,
scoffing a brimming bowl of cereal,
toast and jam ready, the next course,
waiting in front of her.

'This camp food's fantastic,' she says.
'Oh, and don't bother calling me Henrietta,'
she warns. 'Plain Hen will do.'

Alex looks up to laugh but like Hen
her mouth is too full of food.
You can't see where it goes on Hen –
she's as thin and long as a brolga.

How can I begin to compare?
These girls who look so right.
I'm the impostor here, surely.

On the opposite bench

the senior rowers are talking of travel.

'Where're we off to in April?' one asks.
'It should be windy Wendouree, but now?'

'Where's that?' I whisper to Sarah,
reach for more stewed apricots
and a second helping of Sultana Bran.

'You know, it's the old Olympic venue.
Ballarat, silly. Haven't you been anywhere?'

Softly, I sing my reply,
mimicking the ad campaign,
'Short holidays, short holidays.'

The seniors look across at me
as if I'm deranged
so I just eat for a while
before talking again.

I add, 'I've never been out of South Australia,'
and, I think to myself, have hardly travelled
beyond Semaphore, or the Port, and now
one small part of the foothills.
Then I realise, at least now I'm seeing the Murray.

'Not just the seniors travel,' says Sarah,
'but us as well, the juniors, we get
Canberra in the spring term,' she finishes.

'You two, too,' Alex tells me and Hen,
'if you're still crazy enough
to be doing this then.'

'I don't think anyone'll be going
or rowing on Lake Wendouree,' sighs Sarah.
'I heard my dad tell my brother
the course's closed down.'
She looks across the bench to the seniors
and says it loudly so they can hear.

'The drought's dried it up.
You couldn't paddle across it
even if you wanted to.
There are paddocks growing there now.'

I quickly learn

what a typical camp day is like:

Up at five to a racket of birds,
race for the showers (probably cold),
then a warm-up – the obligatory five-k row
up the river while it's flat, then back.

Food for breakfast,
food for lunch,
at night almost too exhausted to eat
but do so, anyway,
knowing the next morning
starts with the row
then the training run
again and again.

Learning how to get in boats,
the different sorts of boats,
where to sit
and how to hold the oars.

Watching the others
– who know what they're doing –
trying to imitate them,
copy the way it's done.

Finally dropping into bed
when the day is through.

Last night of the camp

and I'm really whacked.
Never before have I felt
so exhausted.
But my mind's a whirl,
my brain spinning
not slumping to rest
in tune with my deadweight body.

The others are restless
in their bunks too,
and we start talking.

'These big runs are nothing
for my brother,' says Sarah.
'When he rowed for the state,
he used to wake four times a week
at four a.m. and every night
run for at least an hour.'

She tells us how her father
rowed when he was young
then insisted his two children row
whether they wanted to or not.

'He's so nostalgic for the old days,'
she says. 'When he dropped me off
and saw all the oars stacked
neatly in a line by the river bank,
he jumped out of the car
to unload the boats.'

'Maybe he should help out more,'
Alex mimics a coach's voice.
'Or take up rowing again himself.'

I get the feeling she doesn't approve
of parental influence like Sarah's dad's.
She seems more independent,
a self-starter.

Outside, the wind is getting up,
soughing through the willow branches,
muffling the sound of cars
retreating in the distance.
A weird hooting comes from close by.

'What's that?' I ask, spooked.

'An owl, stupid,' says Alex.

From her top bunk, Hen pipes up,
'It's a mopoke. That's not really an owl
but it looks like one and sounds
sort of similar.'
'Enough of the biology lesson!'
complains Alex. She adds,
under her breath, though I can hear,
'Miss know-it-all.' Out loud again,
'It's time to sleep.
Don't forget we've got the regatta.'
Alex says it like it's final.
'And they call it the Fun Regatta!'
Hen is unbelieving, laughing.

But my brain must eventually
catch up with my sleeping body
'cos the next thing I know
it's morning.

Right from the start of the Fun Regatta

Hannah is yelling, 'Row harder!'
You wouldn't believe such a loud noise
could come from a girl so small.
Her heart-shaped face looks angelic
but her voice is a devil's.

Wind whips waves across the river,
drops fly into my eyes,
catch in my throat.
I gasp for breath.

'Stroke… Stroke… Stroke!'
As our cox, Hannah is trying,
establishing a rhythm for us.
With only Hen and me as newbies,
the other six seem at least to know
what they're doing.

We're racing as an octascull,
like the usual rowing eight
but for stability using two oars each
not one.

In this race, we're up against
two senior crews, coxless pairs
with only two rowers to a boat.

Both boats have already caught up
like terriers, nipping at our heels.
'Watch your lift at the bow, number three.'
That's my position, but I have little idea
what Hannah means me to do.

My feet slide, scrape, and my arms haul
muscles taught as rope.

I keep my eyes ahead
but can barely focus.
Water splashes as the boat
skips through small waves.

'Three-hundred-metre mark,'
calls Hannah, face angelic no longer
but red as a lobster
painted on a chip shop window.

'Third of the way through.'
Hannah is unrepentant.

Only a third?
How can I keep going?

In the middle of the regatta

my mind is wandering.
I'm thinking about the camp,
how I've managed to bond quickly
with rowers across the years
from a school I've not yet started.
I think of the sun –
how, when it set on the second day,
the coaches, most past Acacia rowers,
jumped into the water with some of us
to cool down.
I try not to think about my blisters,
how I know they must be burst and bleeding,
how my back aches
and my backside has stiffened
into an insoluble lump.

Then to my left
one of the senior crews slows.
Bit by bit
their boat falls behind.

'Yeah!' Alex grunts.

'We're two lengths ahead!' Hannah screams.

'Harder, crew. We have a chance!'
Her voice is raw. 'C'mon, crew. Hold the advantage!
We can do it!'
Can we possibly beat them?

And still the race is going

'Catch! Away! Up the rate!'
Hannah urges.
In unison our sixteen blades
dip into the murky water,
turn, and together lift out.

It's the halfway point
and I feel queasy.
My muscles begin to quiver,
my stomach lurches.

Should I have eaten so much
before the race?
Our coaches said to stuff ourselves
full of as many carbs as we could take.
For lunch I had a baked potato
with the lot, that's lasagne, as a topping.
Then it was the healthy stuff –
fruit pudding, jelly and ice cream
– all like heavy rocks landed in my guts.
Will I pass out? Vomit?

Only about a hundred metres left.
One pair is lengths ahead,
the other crew, in small jerks,
is catching back up
and pulls alongside.

Then I can't take it any more

I moan, 'No more.'

But Hannah is relentless.
'You can do it.
We can do it.
Stroke.
Stroke.
Lift the rate!
Make a last dash!'

I can hear her voice
is giving out on her.

But we can't give in,
can't give up.
Must.
Keep.
Going

Then we're across the line.

'Yes,' she croaks.
'We've done it!'

The race is finished.
We've beaten one crew.
The first boat never to be beaten by us
yet we manage one.
Not by far, but by far enough.
So not come last.

We draw up beside the winners.
They're grinning.

At stroke position, frontmost in the boat,
Sarah slumps forward.
Domino effect we follow,
Alex, me, Hen and the others.
We can't speak.

Then I raise my head.
I rasp, 'What
have I got myself
in for?'

No one
is able
to answer.

When Mum and Sammy pick me up

for a minute I realise
I've forgotten about home

and the way the car should be headed
all the way down the Freeway
then off to the horizon
where the silver sunset water
lies ahead,
a beacon and a pathway,

not turning off, as we do,
cutting through
the winding way
through the Hills

to the art teacher's
residential house
of damp air and rattling trains,
where I feel so disconnected
from my old life and friends
I could just sink and go under.

Day One

at Acacia High and I'm lost.
Everyone else seems to know
where to go, what to do.
Following my nose is turning out trickier
than at training camp.

Here the big E-shaped building
is a maze where stairs lead nowhere
or to restricted staff zones.
That isn't counting
the extra temporary rooms
or ovals and quadrangles
upon ovals and quadrangles.

Despite a hurried meeting with my class teacher,
Mr Matieson, and sitting in my first home group,
all is confusion. Though I probably
spoke to someone somewhere, it's a hazy memory.
I'm in a class with a teacher who's talking
a gazillion kilometres an hour
surrounded by conscientious students
their heads down, taking notes.

I'm trying to make sense
of a subject I couldn't care less about.
Just when I think I'm feeling
hollow enough to faint,
another bell rings and I realise I'm hungry.
At least it's lunchtime.

In the canteen's chaotic line-up

I feel a tug at my skirt
and turn to find Hen.
I have to laugh.
Her skirt hangs nearly to her ankles,
covers her skinny legs.
Already she has a pen stain on her shirt.

'At least you know how to tie
a really great knot,' I say.
'I struggled with mine this morning.'

At Lighthouse High I wore jeans and a tee
where the uniform was never a big deal.
Here, there's so much literature about
the correct items of clothing.
I thought it must be a joke but Mum said not,
told me I should see what kids have to wear
at her private school.

Matieson's already pointed out
the detention code if I don't get it right.
He said he thought it'd do me good,
smarten me up a bit. Huh.
Worst thing, I had to ask Mum
how to tie my tie.

'This is crap,' I tell Hen,
fingering the knot.
She twangs hers out –
it's on sewn-on elastic!
Then she gives me a little shove
– the queue's moved.

'C'mon, TC. Order your food,'
she grumbles. 'I'm starved.'

'You're always hungry!' I say.
At the training camp Hen ate
what I did and half as much again.
Like a beanpole you couldn't fill up.

We don't spot any rowers
in the oily chips and meat pie
hot crush of the canteen
so we head out across playing fields
to the back edge of the school,
where we settle under a large tree.
Gums line the oval with a pergola-type thing.
Seats underneath are already stacked
with noisy students.
We sit quietly eating the pizza slices,
watch groups on the grass
yelling and playing games.

Then another bell rings.
I can't believe it –
lunch is over already
and I have to face more strange classes.
Would drag my feet but
Hen's pointed out her home group
and it isn't too far from mine.
With a quick flick of a smile,
she's gone, swallowed up by the tide.

The amount of books

I've been lugging, Mum complains
they're too heavy for me.
Why so many, anyway?
How can you read that much?
What do they expect there?

There are my fees to organise,
all sorts of notes to bring home,
and every day, the planner to fill in.
That's confusing in itself.
Why's my diary called a planner?
Mum always said anyone who has to fill one
should have their head read.
Why be so bogged down? Just hang loose.
Now even she is overwhelmed
filling in her own school's planner.

At Acacia everyone seems obsessed with study.
The whole school has a reputation,
so they bang on at assembly.
Hardly a fortnight of being a student
at this esteemed institution and
I've already had it drummed into me.
The scholastic aptitude of our students.
The merits of our graduates. Blah blah.
Famous politicians who came from this school.

Why does everything have to be
so high pressure?

Our home group teacher, Mr Matieson,
so far's managed to put in
the fear of imminent failure
each home group period.

A beach babe knows all this, doesn't she?
You can keep up, can't you?

Not that it's the same twenty minutes each day.
Home group time differs,
according to the day.
Remembering when we have double lessons
or singles, can leave early,
or have to remain, is whacked.

It's like I'm switched on to a test pattern
or static until further notice.

At change-over time

from Science to Society and Environment
on the next Wednesday of term
it all gets too much.

My brain's in a whirl.
None of the rowing crew
is in that class and
not one soul has spoken to me,
even acknowledged that I exist.
At all.

What am I doing at this school anyway?
Why was it me who had to move?
Couldn't I catch trains to Lighthouse High?
There, where I know the score,
what to do, who to know,
why to do it. Or not.

I throw my folders and books
onto a seat between two buildings,
slump down beside them.
Right now I'm not going anywhere. Won't budge.
Around me, students are whizzing from class to class,
a frenzy of activity.
Green skirts swirl in the air, grey pants sway,
white shirts flap, like washing on a line.

I am sitting still, just sitting.
Why should I move?

A seagull squawks overhead

and I think, *A seagull, this far from the sea?*
My old school was always filled with those birds.
Is always filled. Right now, the Year 10s
would be preparing for the first term rave.
Lighthouse small enough everyone knows everyone.
Here, I'm aching for a familiar face.
Bailey and Ant, even Fish would do.
Truly.

Schoolwork isn't such a production number there.
No pressure at all.
I remember Bails and me, hanging out, maybe swimming.
Still soaking wet after crashing about in the waves,
throwing seaweed at each other,
we'd go buy triple scoops,
drip salt water,
melting ice creams,
through the streets.

Acacia's thousand-plus population
more than quadruples Lighthouse's.
This campus a labyrinth
beyond my comprehension
finding the path through.

Well, not today.
My legs have rebelled, gone on strike.
So I just sit, take stock.
Then I feel as if the weight of my books,
expectations of teachers merging,
crushing down on my shoulders.
I swipe at my pile of stuff,
watch it topple to the asphalt.

My planner skids into the path of a small boy,
obviously only a Year 8,
tripping him as he rushes for his next class.

'Hey! Get a grip, why don'tcha?'
He boots the planner back at me,
catches me on the shin.
I pick it up and sit it on my lap
then open it.
The answer lies in here,
I think, *somewhere.*

Then I take out a black Texta
from my pencil case,
scribble out my doodles
– birds wheeling in a sunset.

In a quiet lunchtime

Hen folds her long arms
around her knobbly knees
and tells me why she's come to Acacia.

'We're what they call blockies
in the Riverland. Mum and Dad
grow apricots, though it's been
more than tough
with the drought.'

She screws up her face
like she's ready to cry.
'That's what we thought, that Dad
was so tired because of no rain
and how hard it was.'

She tells how when the GP tested
they drove straight to town
to run a course of tests.

'Mum's so busy on the block,
said I was underfoot,
that Dad needed me close
to take care of him,
so we're staying with my auntie.
She's the one who knows Shelley,
why I'm here, why I'm rowing.'

She looks at the ground.
'I really want to prove
I'm not in the way,
can do something on my own.'

Hen recovers from her long speech
looks up, across the oval.

'My area school's really different.
This place's a shocker for homework.
I hadn't realised it before –
we pretty well had it easy
where I'm from.'

You and me both, babe,
I think.

February

At our first training session

the two coaches give
Hen and me the standard prelim lecture.
The more experienced rowers
wander through the boat shed
excited as kids at a birthday party.

'Knowing all the proper names
of the boat's parts is important,'
Joe says, as if by rote.
'Then everyone on board will know
exactly where is being referred to.'

He's giving us a serious look
the I'm-a-forthright-professional-here look.
'I'll test you next week,' he warns,
and scratches his nose.

Shelley starts with her big white smile,
tries a more gentle approach.

'You should remember most of this
from the camp, hey?'

I don't. Hen raises her eyes at me
and clearly doesn't either.

Shelley is sweet enough
to take us through it again.

'The seat's on a slide,
sometimes called runners.'
She demonstrates on a boat
in its cradle in the shed.

'See, you can take a longer stroke
using a moving seat.
The front and back ends of the slide
are called the frontstop,' she laughs,
'and, of course, the backstop.'
'And the rigger makes the boat wider,
gives it effective leverage,'
Joe adds, leaning over.

'You put your oar through the swivel.
The gate pin keeps it in place.
See, it's the point of contact
between the blade of the oar and the boat.'

'Blade?'

'Yep. Top, wide part of the oar.
Then there's the shaft, sleeve and collar,
and handle. Got that?
Only the blade goes in the water.
The resistance you exert on the blade
makes the boat move through the water.'

Hen gives me a look that says,
'All this talk is making me dizzy.'
She pulls two muesli bars from her bag,
hands me one.
'Mmm, this stuff's all expensive,' Hen says.

'We don't have so many carbon fibre hulls
wealthier schools can afford.
But what we do have still costs the earth,
would be difficult to replace.' Joe glowers at us
with his big brown eyes, mock-friendly,
waggling his bushy eyebrows.

Shelley smiles again and nods.
'Because the equipment's so dear,
you really need to know how to use it.
Properly. Just one poorly carried boat
crashed coming out of a boat shed
would cost us a fortune.'

'So my rule is this,' says Joe,
emphasising each word:
'Always make sure there are
enough people to lift the boat.'

Our provisional camp squad wander over.

'You don't want to hurt other rowers,' Sarah says.

'Or wreck the boats!' adds Alex.

You can tell they've heard it before.
Shelley is apologetic.

'You won't believe how many people
don't think ahead…'

Joe's on a roll

'Okay, now, really.
Down to the serious stuff.
I want you to pay attention
for the capsize drill.'

He stands in front of us
like a movie airline host.
'Rule number one: don't panic.
Buoyancy chambers on the boat
keep it afloat,
help it right itself if overturned.

'Rule two: leg kick.
A good one'll put your boat
the right way up.
Then reach for the front rigger
while you stand on the rear rigger.
Pull it over and swim or walk with it to shore.
Never lose contact with the boat.
Remember, the cox is in charge,
gives you orders about moving the boat.'

He scowls at us. 'Always,
always, listen to your cox.'

Hen sounds excited.
'Oh, let's get into the blessed boat!'
And I don't know if she's joshing with him
or for real.

Before any real boat work

Joe gather all the rowers
jostling around the boat shed
Acacia shares with City Central.

Hen asks Joe, 'What's that thing called
where you get thrown out of a boat?'

I push forward to listen to the reply.

'I heard the seniors on camp
whispering about crabs…
or something,' Hen adds.

'A crab?' Joe grins.
'You needn't worry about them.'

'Dad's warned me about them,' says Sarah,
acting all-knowing. 'Catching a crab's
when the oar slips out of your hand.
It's uncontrollable
'cos the water catches it
so fast the oar goes vertical
and snaps.'

'Unless you grab it first,' Joe corrects her.

Alex pipes in, 'But that's highly unlikely.'

Sarah dips her head
looks straight at me and Hen.
'The other way's when you're going to the catch.'

She flings her arms out in front of her,
pretends to draw oars toward her,
'And you have feather blades
but when you go to square 'em
you don't square enough…'

'Then, pshtt!' finishes Alex.
'You're out and into the drink.'

When you realise what training entails

Hen seems nervous.
I wonder whether
starting a sport midstream
will be too difficult.

While we wait near the River Torrens's edge,
Alex reaches down and starts touching her toes,
counts to twenty. She stretches up,
her stocky body broader than ours.

'Let's get on with training,' she says,
begins star jumps on the spot.

Joe yells, 'Okay, you guys. All's in order.
Let's begin with a bridge weir!'

A groan goes up from the ranks.

'Well, hey, I expect you to get even better sooner,
then we'll progress to zoo weirs.'
Joe waggles his eyebrows up and down.

I must look dumb, so one of the girls
I recognise from the camp
sets me straight. 'He means running, twerp.
Between the University Bridge and here
or further around to the Zoo,
then around to the weir, and back here.'

'That's gotta be at least three ks,'
a Year 8 junior says.

'More,' qualifies Sarah.

'I'm not that fit,' I admit to Hen.
On top of a hard day at school,
I wonder if I have it in me.

'Then, the ergo machines.' Joe relocks the shed.
'Now let's see how good that training camp
was at preparing you for fitness,
and this.'

He takes off at a jog
and all I can do
is follow.

The weir's a strange place

Joe says without it
there would be no Torrens Lake
for us to row
and the *Popeye* couldn't operate.

As we run towards it, I think
how monstrous it looks.
Jogging across its narrow path
I see the drop, metres down, to rocks.
Stagnant pools dot the lazy flow beyond.
Below that, the water's a piddling creek.

Joe tells us the weir was built in the 1930s.
The whole area feels dark, ugly, scary.
There's rubbish collected all around.
Reed beds are filled with hamburger wrappers.
Ducks honk and there are splashes.

'Erk! Are those rats?' Hen then tries
covering up, and laughs.
'Along with crabs, too?'

'Water rats,' huffs Alex,
running alongside her
unperturbed.

Joe says with a seriously voice,
'I caught a crab real bad once.
Just like you said earlier, Sarah.'
He sounds rueful. 'I sailed
out of the boat
slap into West Lakes.'

'Did it hurt?' I ask, between puffs.

Sarah asks at the same time, 'When was that?'
''Twas like yesterday.' Joe blinks
and adds quickly, 'Head of the River.'

'Oh, I'm so stressed out
about the Head!' cries Sarah.

Behind us are the girls who called me a twerp.
'They shouldn't be worrying about the HOR,'
says one. 'Should they, Scarlett?'

'Nah,' Scarlett replies. 'Not yet, Phoebes.'

'There's more to worry about.'
Phoebe hoots. 'Like their first real race
at this weekend's regatta.'

'Remember our first real race?'

'Yeah, you couldn't keep time.'

'You cracked your blade.'

I turn to watch as Scarlett
growls at her friend.

Phoebe brays a laugh.
'And you slid off your seat!'

Joe glares around at them.
'Between you two
you cost the school
a small fortune,' he says.

He nods to the back group,
sets off on the final leg of the jog
round the river's path
back to Acacia's boatshed.

Hen and I are either side of him,
me puffing, Hen just lolloping along,
and he tells us, 'Remember
if you get to race this Saturday
you'll be facing your first race as novices.
Most of the others across the other schools
will have at least a two-year lead on you.'

I glance over at Hen,
see her eyes widen.

'You'll make it up and don't need to fret.
Anyway, just remember. You're beginners.
Don't panic too much.'
Then he surges forward,
takes way-out lead of the pack.

Behind us, the two girls hiss.

'Ignore them, Hen and TC,' says Sarah,
now at our side.
'It's good we have new members.
We need you for our crew.'

'Yeah, they're just jealous,' says Alex.
'We have the honour of breaking you in.'
She turns her head and speaks louder.
'No one would trust them with a thing.'

'But we'll be there Saturday.'
Scarlett curls her lip
in the prettiest of sneers.

Phoebe backs her up.
'Watching how you'll go at West Lakes.'

West Lakes itself

is reclaimed swampland.
Last year my old gang did a project
on urban planning for Civics.
It's my old stamping ground –
well, down the road a bit.
A development with its own recreated waterway
edged by a fancy suburb,
famous for Football Park
and a shopping mall.
Huge houses line the banks,
some even with their own private piers
like Bec and Lleyton's place, up for sale.

Most regattas on the rowing calendar
will be held here,
though we'll try some other venues
through coming weeks.

Shelley explains it all
driving me and Hen down
from the foothills to West Lakes.

Hen's auntie arranged it
when she heard Mum was busy
marking her first batch
of senior students' essays.

I'm torn between wishing she could come
and glad she and Sammy can't
for my first official race.
And I haven't told Bailey, either.

Once we troop the long hike
from car park to regatta site,
Shelley goes to find Joe.
They assemble all girl rowers
behind Acacia's tent,
where boats are being unloaded
from trailers onto waiting cradles.

'Righto, you lot. Gather round,' says Joe.
'It's time to announce the teams.'

Shelley interrupts. 'Only trial, for today.
We'll see how you go.'

'And let you know after the regatta
who'll be where. Okay?'

I look at the ground.
Who am I to say where I'll be or who with.
But of course I'm hoping.
When I asked at the training
how the choices would be made,
Sarah told me.

'Based on our scores
from ergometric fitness machines,
whether we'd work well together,
But who knows what else,'
she said.

When my name isn't called

for the B team,
I'm concentrating hard.
Will I make it to any team at all?
I must be a reserve,
that's all there is to it.

Joe is very businesslike.
'A team: Alex, Sarah, Hen and...TC.'

I can't believe it, let out a whoop.

'Coach, who's our coxswain?' Hen asks.

'A coxswain'll be needed for each of Acacia's crews.
Your quad's cox, like other crews' ones,
will come from anywhere in Year 8, 9 or 10.
It just depends on the day and the schedule.'

I hear from the others about how coxes
have to be small and light,
be good with throwing their voices loud and clear.
Rich schools might have boats
rigged with microphones and speakers
but we won't have one of those.

'Dad thought I'd make a good cox
when I was younger,' admits Sarah.

Alex looks her up and down. 'I mean, I'm bigger
but you're pretty big, you know.'

'Sure, don't I know,' sighs Sarah.
'Don't think my brother doesn't rub it in,
so I give him back, good as I get
– one of my muscle punches.'
She demonstrates.

'Can't wait to meet him,' Alex says dryly.
'He sounds very supportive of you.'

'No, no, Dylan's really great.
You know, it feels a bit like
him and me versus Dad and Mum sometimes.
They're a bit clingy, you know.
That's why I miss him so much.
Hope he comes home from the AIS,
sees us race sometime.'

But I'm not worrying whether any brother or not
throws punches or not, or can come and see us row,
I'm thinking of Hannah.

On the camp as our cox she was so good
turning us around, helping us dodge other boats,
keeping our steering straight.
I credit her and her demon voice
with fast-tracking my rowing education.

And I've made it to my first team.
A quad. 'A' quad!

There's not long to wait

for our first of two races
on our first real day.
I still have so much to learn.
Now, when someone says,
'I've got butterflies in my stomach,'
I'll know what they mean.
I blame Scarlett and Phoebe
blabbing about their first wrecked regatta.

Only when we're older will we officially row –
that is, use one oar each
alternating bow and stroke side.
Meantime, our rowing'll be really sculling,
using two oars each,
more stable for us juniors.

I try hard not to worry, but
the way it works is
the harder you try
the worse it becomes.
Looking back, how I felt before the Fun Regatta,
was relaxed, compared to how I am now.
Training on the Torrens
was a Sunday picnic.
Nothing has prepared me for this.
The sun is shining,
the water's shining,
and standing at our boat with us,
coach Shelley has eyes that are shining.
'I remember my first race
as if it were yesterday,' she says.

'No, you don't,' counters Joe.

'Of course I do and you weren't there,
so how can you say that?'

'I was there,' he retorts.
'Somewhere…'

Shelley turns to Sarah, Alex and me
while Hen is off taking her third toilet break.
'Don't listen to him.
Joseph's got Oldtimer's disease.'

'You're both just uni students,' says Alex.

'Yeah, but I'm doing Education Honours
and she's only a third year,' says Joe.
He winks at Hen when she returns.

Shelley can't stop beaming at us.
'I know you'll do really well.
Just remember to focus your breathing
and don't tense up.'

'And now,' says Joe, 'as your more senior coach,
with only ten minutes' time
to get down to the start line,
I say go get your boat
and go get into that water!'

Before we touch the boat

Hen briefly takes our hands.
She looks serious as she says to us

– and I think she must be channelling
my hippie mum –

'This will give you energy.'

We stand for a second in a circle
holding hands.
Then our appointed cox, Leah, joins us.

Responsible for how we lift
and move the craft,
she meets our gaze.

'On three.
Two, three…'
she says.

'Lift evenly!' bellows Alex

I gasp. Ours, the *Jonathon Buck*,
is Acacia's oldest but heaviest boat.
Wooden, to be used by beginners
till they're good enough
for the better, faster, lighter,
more expensive boats.

'Named after the patron parent,'
Sarah explains. 'Dylan told me,
'cos he knew the son, who'd rowed elsewhere
and Buck decided it'd be good
for his daughter too, so he fundraised,
and set up Acacia club's
girls' teams along with the boys'.'

Hen stumbles at the narrow concrete path
next to the shore
and the four of us struggle
to maintain balance of the boat.

The crowd is bigger
than I'd imagined it'd be.
Along the grass beside the shore,
competing schools' tents are pitched.

Banners are hammered into the soil
all along the grass bordering the beach,
students and parents sit in deckchairs.
Barbecues are fired and eskies being raided.
Already stands are flogging their wares.
And the tournament is about to commence
at the medieval joust,
my over-drive imagination sings.

Nearest Acacia's plot of bank
with its colours of grey-green and yellow
stands an enormous maroon marquee.
There, lots of parents jostle noisily.

'That's Rutherglen College,' Sarah tells me.
'Don't worry 'bout them.
They fancy themselves enough.'

'Omigod!' I'm gobsmacked,
and let it out without thinking,
'That's the school
where my mum works!'

Alex glares

'Yeah, right,' she says.
'Meanwhile, I'm worried
we haven't smoothed out our strokes.'
She looks across the boat
at Rutherglen's area.

'But you've been practising enough!' Sarah laughs.
'I've noticed. You're just like Dylan,
always bending your wrists up and around.
He even does it at the dinner table
with his knife and fork.'

I feel eyes upon us
as we struggle with the heavy boat
past the grand maroon marquee.
Rutherglen supporters sit in their deckchairs,
eating, I'm sure, cucumber sandwiches.
With ice buckets stacked on plaid rugs,
their chatter is bubbly like champagne.
I look sideways at Hen
then forward at Alex and Sarah.
They back towards the water's edge.

'Watch the rigging!'

'Watch the ground!'

'Hey,' I say, 'don't trip me up.'

'On three,' says Leah. 'Two, three.'
'Lower evenly…' Alex's voice
sinks with the boat.

We ease the boat
smoothly into the water.

Now all that remains
is to get into it evenly.

At the start line

the atmosphere is serious.
We are all too nervous to speak.
Those stories are haunting us
or maybe it's just Scarlett and Phoebes's hex.
Why they should have us rattled, I don't know.
The other rowers in the club
aren't ever mean or unwelcoming.
They're really supportive.
I am worrying I'll be the one member of the crew
responsible for some dire crisis
that will embarrass us all.
Fears of catching a crab hang over me
like a cloud fit to burst.

The start line feels a long way
from everyone else.
It's a busy enough place, though.
There are officials – in speedboats
and on the shore behind the rocks.
To one side of us is a pontoon sort of boat
with one barrel-chested man in particular
who doesn't seem too friendly.
He appears angry
but is it our business to respond?
We are guided by our cox,
who herself isn't sure.

He's shouting through his loudspeaker
'Are…you…ready?'
We don't realise
he does mean us.
He waves his black Greek-captain's hat in the air.

All the other crews are lined up.
Leah has to guide us to the far lane.
She tries to calm us.
Tells us everything will be okay,
she'll keep us in a good line.

'Are you ready?' the official shouts,
cap clapped back on his head again.
Then, 'Row!' he calls.

And we are off.
The sheer thrill of the race
gets me going,
keeps me going
for a while.

Soon, my heart races faster
than I realise it can.
Breathing is what I concentrate on.
Breathing, lifting my shoulders,
driving with my legs.
Catching the water with the oar blade
then withdrawing it away from the water.
Over and over and over.

We are racing a thousand metres.
By only the magic three-hundred mark
my arms already ache. My legs ache.
My eyes swim from the sweat pouring
down my forehead into them.
I squint, try to keep my eyes focused,
try to concentrate on what the others are doing.

I watch Sarah at stroke,
am guided by her and the cox's calls.

I am rasping at air,
sucking it down into my lungs,
then blowing it out, grunting almost.
From a field that began together,
we are steadily dropping behind.

Why I suddenly think of Bailey, I don't know.

I can't tell what we are doing that isn't working.
We're all hauling and shoving,
breathing and trying.
Somehow we're not all getting it together.
We drop further behind.

Our company wears the same colours.
Acacia Bs are beside us.

The two teams are flunking it for the school.

When it's clear we'll never have a chance
of making it up to Rutherglen and City Central,
we fall even further behind.
Acacia Bs drop away at an angle.

The blisters on my hands sting,
my chest is stretched.
With quivering arms,
we return the boat to its cradle.
'Hey, guys. It doesn't matter,'
Joe says as we pull into shore.
'You did well just finishing.'

'Yeah, right,' Alex says under her breath.

And I can't help but worry
it did matter
and somehow
I was the problem.

The rest of the day

on a rocky outcrop near the water's edge
other Acacia rowers watch the races.
Our quad goes to sit with them,
girls and some of the senior boys.
Among them, a handsome one named Nick.

Here we are, I think, new, untried,
untested recruits with the pros.
Coming nearly last.
I'm still too pumped,
have rowed my first official race
to remain dejected.
But I feel the challenge.
Is this something I can rise to?

Two hours later,
once again Rutherglen wins and we lose,
but not so badly.
In the front of the station wagon
on the return journey
I ask Shelley how the Bs went.
I never did find out.

'Oh, they did fine,' she says.
'Off course and out of the first race
then the same for the next.
But you all did so well
I'm proud of you.'

It's the end of the day.
I can hear my tummy rumbling.
Before the race, going on what I'd learnt
from the cramps in the camp's 'fun' regatta,
I'd been too nervous to eat.
After the race I'd been too grateful
just finishing to go look for food.
We hadn't disgraced ourselves.
Of course, we'd finished last.
But we'd finished without mishap.
I was so relieved.

'Like some jellybeans?'
Shelley points to the glovebox.
'My secret stash of energisers.'

Four-wheel drives towing trailers
laden with our boats lead the Acacia convoy.
Near Westfield Marion we become stuck
in a line waiting for a train to pass the level crossing.
In clogged traffic I see shoppers
impatient to get home.

Ours is a long journey back along the coast
and up and into the foothills.
While Hen dozes in the back,
Shelley glances across at me.
'Today went great, especially the senior girls' eight.
They're really buzzing.'

A double-carriage passenger train rattles past
then the boom gates begin to lift.
Shelley turns back to the road.
'And you never know. The Year 10 A quad
might just acquit itself.'
She turns the radio on to Triple Z.
Then she adds, 'In the big event.'

'Which is?'

'Head of the River.
Don't you know
that's the biggest gig of all?'

I thump my hand to my forehead.
I should know.
But then what do I know?
I feel an enormous yawning emptiness
open inside me – all there is to recall
and remember in this new sport.
So I listen to the soft music
the rest of the way home
– lyrics about broken love.
I'd welcome even a broken love right now,
I think, *ahead of no love at all.*
But then again,
maybe not.

That night I dream

Mum's favourite TV drama hero
Horatio Hornblower
is looking over his brig,

a swag
roped at his feet.

He turns to me,
eyes pleading,

then I step onto a tram
and it pulls away

but suddenly I'm flying
over the ocean

merely a bird,
alone in the sky,

a speck of a ship
heading into a storm
way below.

Next week

Mum comes home trilling with the goss –
'A Rutherglen benefactor just donated
a slap-bang brand-new fancy rowing boat
for the junior girls quad.'

'Typical.' I know it was a mutter
and I can feel my scowl.

Mum does a double take
'Oh, my little Tabby Cat,
I'm sorry. I didn't think.
I'm all a bit aflutter today.'

Her red frizz is looking a bit better today.
I notice the streaks of grey are gone,
the red's less coppery.
Come to think of it,
she's toned down the whole hippie make-up
and, since working at the school,
seems to have smartened up her act.

'Tell me about your rowing.'

Where do I start? Do I tell her,
It's consuming my life.
I never knew a sport could be like this.
I live for training
and thrill more deeply to my races
than I ever believed possible.
Could I have guessed I liked to try so hard
at some – thing?
Was making a big effort?

'Yeah,' I admit, 'it's okay.'

'Coaches entered us into races last weekend
and we went well in the first one,
nearly beat Rutherglen to third place.'

'Oh, goody!' She smiles.

I don't admit how we cooled off
after the sweat of the first race,
running into the water,
emerging soaked,
racing the second race
still dripping,
coming last by tons.

'I think we're gonna make it.
Only four more regattas
before the big 'un.'
I add some sparkle with the news
but realise Mum doesn't know
what I'm on about.
'Head of the River. Finale
for the schools' rowing season.'

'Already?' She's amazed.

'Already,' I repeat,
not surprised she's amazed.
I am too.

Bailey telephones

suggests I hop a ride
down to the jetty for a swim
before the hot weather ends.

I explain how my training regime
and the racing program
means I'm struggling.

'But I'm missing ya, mate,
and there's the end of term rave
we're organising…thought maybe
you could come, too.'

'Er, sorry, Bails,
there's this horrendous
overdue homework…'

'Bloody hell, TC!
When did you ever care before?'

When I hesitate with an answer,
the line goes dead.

Well, waa, she was probably only
trying to hook me up with Fish.
Dateless or not,
I'm not that desperate.

March

Shelley balances on her bicycle

next to the boatshed.
'Tonight's the night, girls.
You've had half a season of training.
You're getting used to regattas.
But we need a bit more discipline.
Tonight, I want some real effort.'

She straps on her helmet,
tucks her hair under it.
'And I mean from the heart.'
Her pointed look at each of us
underlines her words.

Shelley straddles her bike.
Since last week she's been
testing our times,
riding beside the river
on the pedestrian path.

Other club coaches use it with their bikes.
Only some private schools afford
coaches in motorboats on the water
cruising next to the rowers.

From bikes, as they ride along,
coaches yell out.
Another club's coach, I saw,
uses a megaphone, unbalanced, wobbling.
Shelley doesn't have one,
though it'd be good
if she did.

None of us likes to tell her
half the time she's yelling stuff out,
we can't hear what she says.

Sometimes she's calling out
but facing the other way.
Other times we can hear her.
'Pull the oars like this' or
'Lift your rate, keep a straighter line'
but her words are only faint,
her voice carried away
across the grass on the bank
not over the water to us crew.

On the banks, the plane trees
look less bleached than in summer
as if with the going of the heat
their colour can return.
Now it's March and officially autumn,
the sun sets earlier.

Golden light
shines into our eyes.

As we row under Princes Bridge

I speak out. 'There are things
I love about rowing and things I hate.'

'What do you hate?' asks Alex,
clearly surprised there could be anything.

'Lack of sleep. That's top of my list.'
If I could get to sleep quickly at night,
maybe the early mornings wouldn't be so hard.

'Yes, exhaustion,' Hen chips in.

'Blisters.'

'Blisters upon blisters.'

'My hands've calloused up already,' says Sarah.
'But I should've guessed that'd happen.'

'See. It's a terrible sport. Such pain!'
I've had such a short time rowing,
sometimes ponder if I can keep going at all.
Not for the first time, wonder
if only I was back with my old gang –
and I know I ache to see Bailey –
then Shelley yells from her bike
and though I'm not sure of the actual words
we all start to pull harder
and lift our rate.

On Sunday morning

Mum calls out from her bedroom.
Blotchy-faced Sammy's
clamped to her ankles.

'Sweetheart, your brother's teething.
Would you be a honey and walk him
round the block, maybe find a swing?'

She's surrounded by folders.
'They're assignments on public sculptures,'
she says, seeming more strained than usual,
so I strap the struggling form
into the pusher,
plop a hat on his head
and set off, singing silly songs.

These foothills alien.
Sometimes, if I'm walking
early enough, like now,
I've even seen kookaburras,
fat and greedy birds
looking more intelligent
than stupid gulls.
Autumn cold coming early here,
at dusk already the smoke of open fires,
eucalyptus and pine.
So different to the Esplanade
where each night we saw the sun set –
fiery balls falling into the gulf waters.
Here, sunset's hidden, behind rail tracks,
hills, housing.

Once I get Sammy home,
Mum feeds him and puts him down to nap.
I'm struggling with my homework again,
long to ask for help with the project
but don't want to bother her.

Mum comes in, stands beside my desk,
the room less stale-smelling now
we've thrown lavender oil around.

'So, you going okay at this?'

'Meh,' I say, prop my worksheet
against my cool lamp – one of the new things
Mum's bought from her wages.
'I've filled in all the spaces in the cross quiz
and started on the drawing. See,
I've sketched a bank of cumulonimbus.'

So far, I think, the work's been as complicated
as special therapy. But if, as Ms Zebedy says,
it's breaking us in gently,
then let her have this. 'First worksheets
then down to the real thing,' she said.
'Group projects. Have to work like a team.
Together, give an oral presentation.
On a theme of your choosing,
so long as it's S and E.'

My group's three no-hoper guys
have done zip so far.
Why should I bust a gut for them?

Not one among them
who can string two sentences together.
Not coherently.
It's dead in the water
before it's even begun
really.

But deep down is the core of my worries
speaking out the front of the class
at a school that's so damned academic,
something I'm so nervous of
and feel complicated about
that it's too hard even to know
where to begin
saying anything to my mother about.

'You can go now,' I tell her.
'You've got your own homework to do.'

Then overnight it seems

the swans are out in force
and have sprung families.
One day just swans,
next minute, hordes of little ones,
the parents possessive of their young.

'They're real Ugly Ducklings, aren't they,'
I nod to the others as our oars dip in time
and we slip past *Popeye's* landing.

'Cygnets,' says Hen, who seems to know
all about wildlife.

'Yeah, TC, get it right.'
Alex always the one to tell me off.

'Oh, they're beautiful,' says Sarah.
'Little balls of grey fluff.'

And I'm a mass of waves of emotion
anyway
catching the train home
as the dark begins to fall.

When I get back home

there's a gar-bag
bundle dumped
on the back step.

I probably wouldn't have opened it
except there's my name
written in Bailey's messy scrawl.

When I open it up,
my heart goes cold
– inside, the soft plushies and the toys,
things I gave to baby Cheri.

I clutch at old Lambkin,
rip open the envelope,
hope for some sort of revelation,
but there isn't even a note.

At the Port River regatta

our coaches agree we're lucky our club
doesn't have to train here.

The water's black underneath and in its depths,
across the surface is a slick.
Scum floats all around.

Coaches and crew,
we stand in our socked feet
at the edge of the at-least-sandy beach
examining the water.
Oily, the yuk soaks in.

Hen stands close to Alex and Sarah
but I feel aloof.
Something's got into me.
I couldn't get to sleep last night
thinking of the toys,
of Bailey's desertion,
the loss of all I've known.

Then couldn't wake this morning.
My limbs feel leaden,
even the prospect of today's race
brings no usual thrill.

Somewhere I've lost my confidence,
now can't believe I'm standing here
in these rowing clothes
getting ready to row a race
for Acacia High.
I feel a fraud, not team-sport material
nor fit, clever or happy.

Why should anyone want me with them?

This is the regatta the quad
was aiming to clinch.
Last training, Shelley said
we were doing great.
She'd clocked us. Said we'd romp it in.
I should feel confident but I don't.

The whole day feels unlucky,
the gloomy river with its tug boats,
industrial wharves,
shipping container warehouses
– weird place.

I sense we don't fit, I don't fit,
that I'm out of sorts with me,
the crew, the surroundings.

Of all the days, this is the one
Mum has driven me down to the regatta
to watch her first race.
I should be grateful she's here with Sammy.
But I'm not appreciating it.

Today is a test for the quad
in advance of trials
to qualify for the Head.
Today we most need to be showing
what a good team we are,
how ready we are
for those important regattas ahead.

But today, I don't belong here.
The others aren't noticing,
but I can feel it, and I'm confused.

I drag myself to the boat for our first race.
Mum smiles, but I can't summon a response.
The boat's so heavy, when I'm in it
I feel heavy myself.

Then, in the race proper,
I'm breathing and straining,
doing the right things with my arms and my legs,
but my concentration's not spot-on.

I'm not living in the rowing moment.

I'm distracted.

And I catch a crab.

So this is it

the water resists my oar,
slams into my chest.
River water sprays me soaked,
and the rest of the crew.
It isn't a bad crab,
I don't fly out of the boat or anything.
But I've wrecked the crew's rhythm,
can't recover mine.

Alex barks at me
as we row back to the shore
from the finish line.
'You were holding the handle
all wrong, you dolt.'

Walking beside me,
I see the cox looking nervous.

Alex saves all her frustration
for me, though.

'You've got the angle on the blade
all over the place.
Couldn't you have focused?'

Sarah avoids looking over at me,
as if there's nothing going on.

As if no one's being bawled out.
On the beachhead, Rutherglen's A quad
is celebrating its third straight outright win.
One of the crew calls out
a greeting to my Mum.

All I need.

We stow the boat.
Alex looks at me.
'They know we're their best competition
that we've com-plete-ly lost it.'
In long strides, she's off
first, Sarah follows,
then, with what looks like a regretful glance
over her shoulder,
Hen takes off after them.

'Hey!' I call out
but none of them turn round.

Mum hoiks Sammy on her hip and walks to me.
She wants to comfort me, I think.
But I don't want that from her.
Not her, not today.

She drives us home,
Sammy sleeping –
silence all the way.

Hen's already on the platform

when I'm at the station after school.
It's a miracle I've dragged myself here,
can summon enough energy to face training.
Hen sits on the wooden bench under the veranda,
reading a book, not looking up or speaking.
I dig into my backpack, get out the water cycle book
– at least it'll help with the S and E oral.
When the train arrives, I feel a skip of fear
as Hen gets on to a different carriage.

I pretend I don't see her at the terminus
and since there's still time before training
I head off for Rundle Mall to go window-shopping.
Whether I am prepared for it or not,
there's a dinner dance at the season's end
and who knows if I can find a dress
to look even halfway decent,
even with no date.

On the way back to the river
I walk up King William Street,
past the Festival Theatre, to the rotunda.
From the tourist motor launch, *Popeye*'s landing,
I head along the bike path to Acacia's boat shed.
Joe's there with Hen, holding her foot behind her,
looking crazily like some flamingo.

'Go on,' says Joe. 'Now TC's here
you can do it with her.'
'What?' I ask.

'You're still early. Remember?
Training's late tonight. I've just told Hen
since she's got the time
she should try taking out a scull.
Now, you can both hop into a double scull.'

Hen, who has still not acknowledged me,
says, 'But I can't do that yet.'

'You can still use two oars each.
They'll keep you steady.'

Hen seems hesitant.

'Come on,' he says, encouraging us,
twitching up his eyebrows.
'It'll be good for your blade skills,
good for building strength,
and best for learning
how to look after yourselves.'

So we do.

'But let's avoid the weir, okay?'
I say to Hen. 'That place terrifies me.'

She half-smiles lopsidedly
and I figure it's a beginning.
Maybe going out on the boat together
will fix things up.

Taking the boat from the rack

is hard with only the two of us,
tricky, as neither of us is
strong like Alex or even Sarah.
So Joe takes one end and together
me and Hen take the other.

'Always make sure there're enough of you
to lift a boat,' Joe says it a word at a time.
'You wouldn't believe how many rowers
hurt themselves or wreck boats
by not thinking ahead
or having enough muscle power.'

Hen catches my eye as we manoeuvre
the bow spit through the shed.
Joe has the stern with its fin and rudder
to worry about, but we're the ones
walking backwards out of the shed.
It's a lovely craft, though.
Much lighter than the *Jonathon Buck*
of course – anything's lighter than that old tub.
It's made of modern materials.
Even its cleats are aluminium.

Once we lower it and ourselves into the river,
we relax a little.
Then it feels like an adventure,
despite the responsibility
of such an expensive boat.
Not that the boat's easy. It's a real challenge.

We warm up with a quick row
down to Community's boat shed
near the weir end of the lake.
After a while we get into the rhythm of it.
We haul together, push our legs together,
dip blades, lift, dip again.

How free to be on the river, I muse.
Just the two of us. No cox, and little communication.
Only the two of us feels very different.
Of all the crew, I suppose it's Hen
I've felt closest to, the other outsider
the freshman, newbie, kid from the country.

We reach Community's shed then turn the boat.
We sit at the catch ready to row back
when we hear them.

We crane our heads around

see the city's tourist boat, the *Popeye*,
that plies its trade up and down the river,
is puttering by, crammed with a raucous crowd
of men dressed in togas.
One of them leans out and shouts at us.

'Oy, lovie, show us ya muscles!'

Hen sucks in her breath.

'Yobbos,' I tell Hen.
'Don't worry. They can't hurt us.'

'What's the *Popeye* doing
filled with them?' she asks.

In the quad, we've often passed the launch
but now the crowd on board makes all the difference.
Usually, it's stacked with tourists or families
on the craft's slow route from rotunda landing to the weir
then down to the Zoo and back again.
Half the time, little kids would lean over the sides,
throw crumbs at the swans,
get dragged back in by anxious parents.

Tonight the crowd is obviously different.
Some music springs up from the boat's front,
from a portable player, booming out rap.
The crowd cheers. I hear chinks of glass.
'Oy, darlin', go on, show us whatcha made of!'

'They're drunk!' I say and bend my head
to concentrate on rowing.

A group gathers round the heckler,
joins him in yelling at us.

I can't say how it happens.
Hen might be distraught but I'm not too upset.
I don't know what we do wrong.
Do our hands let go?
Does one of us unexpectedly lean?
I don't know.

We tip over.

Inside out

tip right over.
Still in our seats with our feet laced
snug into the boat's shoes,
Hen and I struggle to right the boat.
I'm under water and terrified.
My mouth's full, my eyes are a blur,
my head's heavy as a block of ice.
The world feels inside out.

It's all happening as if in slow motion
but we're still turning, turning,
then the boat rights.

What a beauty, the boat rights.
Beautifully.
From relief or something, I don't know,
we begin to splutter laughter.
Our hair's streaming and our clothes are soaked.
How funny, it seems, a dunking in the river.
I splash at Hen with some of the water
lying in the boat.

The *Popeye* has moved on past us
down to the weir
and though there're now no yobbos calling out,
neither is anyone watching over us.

We are still smiling

How cracked to have upended.
What a joke.
Hen's hugging me and I'm hugging her.
We're together. Then, I realise
just how much water
the boat is taking on.

I watch Hen as she realises, too.
See her face go white.

'TC,' she cries, 'we're sinking!'
With arms flailing, she starts to splash around.
'Quick, let's get out of here.'
It's a scream of near-hysteria.

I cup my hands,
try bailing out the water,
but Hen is growing frantic,
not trying to bail at all.
That's when I finally understand.
I read the message in her eyes,
her terror of the water.

I scream at her, 'Can't you swim?'

'No!' She starts to cry.

'Unbuckle your feet,' I instruct her
as if she's a child.
She bends over,
unclasps her socked feet
from the boat's shoes.

'Climb to the spit.'
Hen scrambles to the bow
and my end lists heavily.
I undo my own shoes and look around.

'We'll make for over there,' I say,
pointing to the bank
outside the restaurant
next to the weir.

This is the very weir I fear,
with the water thundering over its ledge,
plummeting down to the rocks below.

I strike my oar into the water
as if I'm punting.
I'm not panicking but I'm really scared.

River water tips right over the weir's gates.
The flow's not massive but it's alarming.
Could we be swept over, too?
It feels inevitable, like canoes over rapids,
or kayaks white-water rafting.
All of a sudden our sport that has seemed
so safe and tranquil is terrifying.

Hen has frozen into a crouch
at the point of boat.
If I don't do something,
water will swamp us.

My lone efforts with the oars

are getting us nowhere.

'Hold on tight,' I say,
take a big gulp of air,
for courage as much as anything,
and, keeping a grip on the edge of the boat,
I slip over the edge.

The water's cold,
a shock to be in its dankness again,
but I edge my way to the end opposite Hen.

In a cross between a paddle and a frog kick,
while grasping the end,
I can somehow tow the boat.

Hen stays, maintains a balance,
still huddled as a new cat
pulled from the safety of a pet shop's carrier.

I'm panting as I go and the going is slow.
I have to control my thoughts
because if I think about the situation
I'll panic, and I can't afford to panic.

In the draining light

the water looks inky
I can feel nameless stuff
brushing against my legs.
What if reeds snag me? Or worse?
I make a line for the shore past the weir.
Reeds choke the banks
but in front of the large double-storey restaurant
there's a clearing and a small wooden landing.
The pathway round the lake is empty,
the *Popeye* long gone.
Where are the people?
No one in the restaurant
or jogging on the path?
I can't believe we're so alone.

With a few more lengths, I finally reach the ledge.
I look back at Hen. Have to think.
Pause a second to collect my breath.
What's going to be difficult,
what I've never tested for myself,
is getting out of the actual river.

How will I get up?

Pulling myself clear of the Torrens
is going to be hard. Harder than I imagine.
My clothes run with the slimy water.
They're so heavy as I heave myself up
I'm dragged back in.

On my second attempt I tell myself
I can do it and with a mighty haul
clear the surface.
As my feet make contact with the planks,
I realise I'm nearly there.

That's when I begin to shake.

Holding tight to the outrigger, I beckon to Hen.
But can I keep it together long enough
to get her out?

'C'mon,' I say

'We're safe now.'
I wait as Hen unwinds herself,
clambers along the boat
out onto the platform.
For a minute she hangs from my neck
in a clinging embrace
then she pulls free.

'Thanks, TC,' she says.

Dripping and shaking, we sit down.
I'm still holding the outrigger,
keeping the now half-submerged boat
from knocking against the tiny jetty.

'What'll we do about the boat?'
Hen is stuttering with the cold.

The boat, low with all the water that's streamed in,
will definitely be too difficult for us to pull free.
Urgently, the water needs complete bailing out
or the boat will sink into the river.

'I'll try to keep hold, Hen.
You run back to the boat shed,
bring back a bucket,' I say.

Hen seems to shake herself,
then without a word,
takes off at a loping run,
leaving a trail of wetness
across the weir's walkway.

'Get Joe!' I call out after her.
Then I watch her on top of the weir
then down to the gravel walkway through the trees
winding down until she's out of sight.

The sky is flaming orange and mauve
– a magnificent sunset.
As I squat holding onto the boat,
I hear noises of the city floating across the water.
Sounds are magnified over waterways.
Stray voices of far-off joggers carry.
From the bridge in the distance,
I hear cars tooting in the going-home traffic.

Through the dimming light I make out Joe
returning with Hen. Between them
they're carrying wooden trestles and buckets.
Without a word, the three of us empty the boat,
rescue it from the river,
stand it on its supporting blocks.
When it's completely drained,
we cart it back to Acacia's shed.

Night is fallen and, like Hen,
I continue shivering.

I open my eyes

and see people standing over me,
peering at me, interested.
I think I might be dreaming.
It sounds like they are on a tour,
with a tour guide, talking,
them taking notes, nodding.
Then the tour guide, I realise, is a doctor
conducting his class.
I'm still woozy, groggy, disoriented.
I'm working out if I actually will chuck up
or whether I should ask for a painkiller.

Mum's beside my bed,
whispers that she's taken the day off work
to spend in hospital with me.

She asks the doctor when he comes to my side,
'So, you think the river water's responsible?'

'Sure thing,' he replies, smiling
more than he should for such a statement.

'For the fever, vomiting and diarrhoea?'

'Patients don't regularly present
having fallen into the Torrens.'
He laughs at his own joke,
'But her symptoms would lead me to believe
that was the cause.'

Surprised, I realise he's flirting with my mother
so I cut in between them, 'But it's still okay
for me to go to training tomorrow?
I mean, I don't think
I'll throw up any more.'

He scribbles on my notes. 'Oh, I think not.
You need a good rest. Let those sores heal, too.'

I look down at my festering scratches.
Somehow, in the process of pulling the boat
from the water, long weals of flesh
were gouged along my arms.

'Antibiotics are for the infection,'
he carefully tells my mother.

Suddenly, I'm desperate.
'What about the regatta on Saturday?'

'Oh, I shouldn't think so.'
He glances beyond me,
twinkles his eyes again at Mum,
who returns a timid smile
then shakes hands with the doctor.

'The drip can come out tonight.
I'll return to look tomorrow,' he says,
then nods at the medical students
and they move on to the next bed
containing Hen.

'He's too young for you,' I tell Mum
as Hen undergoes a repeat procedure.

'I'm not that old, you know.'
She looks down at her hands.
'I'm not too old for him, he's just not my type.
But someone else sometime might be.'

I must grow sleepy and drop off
for when I come-to Mum's gone
and the night nurse is taking my pulse.

'You've done well, ducks,' she says.

'What about her?' I ask of Hen.

'She's not doing so well, I'm afraid.
Probably be here for a bit,' she says.
'Now just let me get this old drip line out, eh?'

'And I can go home tomorrow?'

'Don't know, ducks,
you'll just have to wait and see.'

And I before I know it,
I've sunk into blackness again.

On my first day back to school

after home recuperation,
instead of walking into school
from the Acacia station
I sit down in it.
Pull out from my backpack
my planner, try to orient myself
to the now.
But on the front fly I see my scrawls,
the scribbled cartoon of seagulls
wheeling in the sunset.
The beach, my head sings,
you dumb bunny you, you need the beach.

If there's a rule that says you must go to school
then today it's not the right rule.
Today, school is more than I can handle.
Today, I'll hop off, skip out,
sail my boat to the shore.

My heart is of course jumping its own rope.
(I know this is wrong.)
Mum doesn't know (why will she?)
and the school will only know I'm not there.
I could still be sick. (I do feel sick.)
Sick at heart. So I'll take a sickie.
What do oldies call it?
A mental health day.
You gotta be cut some slack for that
every now and again.
The next train into the station
lets go its passengers – more Acacia students.

I don't board this one –
it will only take me a few more stops.
I'll have to wait for the train to run its course
before the return journey
back into town.

I huddle myself into a corner to wait.
Try not to look conspicuous.

I can't do much about my uniform yet,
but when the train returns
and we're a few stops down the track
I take off my tie and slip my silver locket
over my collar to sit outside my white shirt.

Maybe the tartan green and gold skirt
looks like uniform, maybe it doesn't.

I yank the scrunchie from my ponytail,
let my hair settle over my shoulders.

I look older like this –
lots of blonde hair let loose
has that effect.

I'm still not sure where I'm going
as the train rattles its way through the tunnels
and stations: mine at Torrens Park, then Mitcham,
Goodwood, Keswick, then the city.
In the terminal I look up from the platform
to the electronic boards above.

In five minutes' time there's a train leaving
for Semaphore from Platform 7.
I run for it,
manage to leap on
as the warning bell dings.

Last time I got off

from the Glanville station
Bailey met me with Fish and Ant.
Friends through Seashore Primary
then Lighthouse High.
Why does the thought of her
now fill me with disdain?
It's not her party life, that's cool,
and I stifle the hurt about the toys –
is it that she's got a boyfriend and I don't?

Do I even want a boyfriend?
Who have I ever seen
to really make me want one?
My group's nerds, Tan or Freddy?
Or even any from Acacia at all?
I don't think so.
Half the guys at school don't even wash properly.
Any rowers? We all think Nick's hot.
But he's such a senior, so intent on study,
on winning the first eight.

In hospital again I dreamt of that
handsome vision on two legs.
This time, the air blurred between us
and his eyes
scorched into mine.
But, I admit to myself,
it's more than just a boyfriend
between Bailey and me, isn't it? What?
Face it, you feel excluded.

How much does it take to belong?
I don't think I ask for much.
I'm not bossy or anything,
can be a good friend, I think.

With rowing I wanted to be an insider.
But having caught the crab
in the crucial race,
the others giving me the cold shoulder,
I'm on the outside again
and it hurts.

Then, the accident with me and Hen.
How will that change things?
She should be getting out of hospital today.
Should I call?

The walk down Semaphore Road
takes no time at all.

I'm pacing my way down the asphalt,
not looking in the shops.
Who cares about the shops?
I'm thinking, just thinking.

Feeling outside not inside.
Or stuck between.

Then the smell of the salt water hits me

seagulls wheel overhead.
The bloody seaside.
You can't help it.
You try feeling morose or angry or lost
but you can't keep it up.
Something in the air
lightens your head, swells your ribcage.

I realise my pace is slowing,
I'm breathing deeper, relaxing.

I head straight for the sand.
Off come my socks and shoes,
grains of sand squelch my bare soles.

At the water's edge I stand ankle deep,
small waves lap over my feet,
the tide's on its way out,
only a few fishers heading off.
I clamber onto the jetty,
wander to its end.
It's shorter than it once was
by a couple of storms.
I remember the last one
where Mum had to get cardboard,
jam it hard into window frames
to stop the wind howling through
so I wouldn't think
it was crashing in on me.

After the jetty pilgrimage
I ask I suppose a prayer
of the angel on the memorial –
mute, unformed, I don't know what I ask.

I dare myself down the Esplanade.
Can I do it? Can I go see my house?
Will the family who is renting it be there?
My temples pound as I near.
I count the pine trees from Semaphore Road
south to my place. Then I see it.

The windows are open,
curtains flutter at the sides.
Someone is at home.
Television or radio blares,
and then a woman speaking with a child.
Voices wafting out,
out to me, walking past, listening in.
I keep walking but my head's turned
watching the house, not in front of me,
and I bump slap bang into someone.

'Tabitha!'

'Mrs Dyson!'

'Tabitha!'
She looks me up and down
says, 'Come on in.
I'll get the kettle boiling.'

After sweet tea and fruitcake

our old neighbour looks me up and down again.
'You're different, Tabitha.'

'Mm. Fitter? Rowing, I guess.'
But still me inside, I silent-say.
'I think my friend Bailey
thinks I've changed too much,' I tell her.

'Not that much, surely, dear,' she says.

'It's early home time at Lighthouse,'
I explain, 'so maybe I'll head on there.'

'You do that, Tabitha,
but would you find a way to ask your mother
whether what the letter said
was coming true.'

I give her a hug.
'Sure,' I promise, as I leave,
puzzled how a letter
could say anything true.

A teacher prowling the school's fence
calls out to me. 'Hey, TC,
have you come to move some more tables?'

It's Mr Aird, and, typical,
he's having a dig at me.
'No, seriously,' he says,
'how's the real move been
to the leafier side of town?'

'Fine, I s'pose,' I say.
'Oh, I'm a rower now.'

'Really? My sister did that,
took her all the way to the AIS.'

Then bitch-face Brody glides over
to see what all the excitement is.
But I spot Bailey hanging out at the gate
and rush over to her,
waving Mr Aird a little goodbye,
leaving the gorgon gaping.

'Bails,' I spit out,
bailing her up.
I plonk my backpack in front of her
so she has to stop.

'Yeah? What?'

I push on feeling positive,
smile, and dig into my bag.

'I've got one of Cheri's toys.
I really want her to have it.'

Bailey looks down at the soft lamb
from the returned bundle
then looks up at me
and a small sob escapes.
'Oh, TC, I don't know
what got into me.'

We hug, awkward as a first date,
restful as old friends.

'C'mon, race you to the jetty.
On the way, I'll show you the salon
where Mum's got me a part-time job.'

I stare at her.

'Yeah, I know it's mostly gonna be
blue rinses and perms for the oldies,
maybe some buzz-cuts too,' she looks sideways,
'…for the women who want it that way.'

She shoots me a wicked grin
bumps hips, then yells,
'Race ya!'

So I'm back running down
past the angel on the memorial.

Thank you, I mouth
silently.

The next day out on the oval

I can see now how easy it's been
to be lonely here.
Girls stick to girls and guys to guys.
Back at Lighthouse I was reminded
I had a mixed bunch of friends.
When the girls got too much, sometimes,
it was fun throwing baskets or
booting a footy with the guys.

But I realise my crew here is special.
Rowing's giving me the best of times.

I peer at the closest bunch of guys.
They're the dead-beats
from Society and Environment.

'Hey,' I call. The hacky-sack
rises in the air and Tan snatches at it.

'Yo,' he calls back.

'Come here a minute.'
I unwrap my arms from my knees,
stand and stretch.

He drops the hacky,
kicks it at me.
I toe it up to Freddy.
They move and re-group around me.
We play in silence for a while.
I don't do particularly well.
Then I realise I've been presented
with the perfect opportunity.

'You know our project.'
I mention it casually.
'How we're running out of time…'

Tan frowns. 'Yeah?'

Am I going to blow it?
'I've thought about
what we could do.'

'Yeah?' Freddy's voice squeaks a bit,
but at least he sounds interested.

'How 'bout water quality?
Remember how I was sick for days?
That was from falling in the Torrens.
It's so polluted it made me and Hen sick.'

'In the guts?' asks Brenton.

'Did ya chuck up?' asks Freddy.

'Yep, tons. And the runs.'

'Yuk,' says Tan.

I remember he's a bit soft.
I lift my skirt a little,
show off my legs.
'And my blisters got full of pus.'
I am enjoying this.
'Even the small scratches got infected.
I was really crook.'

'Woah,' they say in unison.

'So we could talk, maybe,
'bout the history of the river,
and what it's like now.'
I smile at them
wiggle my eyebrows up and down encouragingly
like I've seen Joe do.

'I could check out the chemical composition,'
Tan offers. 'My mum works as a chemist
in the Women's and Children's Hospital.'

'Fred, do you think you could find out info, too?
Maybe the part of the question
where it asks about the impact of society?'

'Sure,' he says.

When the bell sounds the end of lunch,
I walk back across the oval.
In the quadrangle I spot the crew.
Hen is pale, but when they see me
they rush over and hug me, squealing.
We're together. Again.

I'm at the kitchen table

the next day after school
with my homework spread both sides of me.
Mum's preparing dinner.

'What?' I say. 'You need a lemon?'

'No, for your oral presentation.
Isn't that what you're struggling with there?'

I am struggling with that.
My S and E has come to this.
But at least now I'm doing something about it.
Tonight I have my books out.
My group is somehow going to have to stand together
perform at the end of the week.
I'm really nervous
feel the taunts of Mr Matieson
in the back of my head.
I think about just winging it,
then remember the Lighthouse gang
mucking around, playing the fool,
and I feel wise enough to realise at Acacia
there'd be no class laughs at any clowning around.
There'd be embarrassment, failure.
And I don't want Zebedy telling Matieson
he's right, I am the dumb beach-bunny
he teases that I am.

Thanks to our last-minute get-together
my group has organised some notes.
But as for how to put it all on as a talk,
my mind's as empty as our biscuit barrel.
I have to come up with something.

'You've got your project material, don't you?'

'I've got all the notes. Tan got stuff from his mum
who's a chemist and I made Freddy and Brenton
sit next to me in the computer room at school
and we all searched the net.'

'So here it is. You say
the three most interesting points.'
Mum looks up from cutting chicken into strips.

'First, introduce what you're going to say.
Then tell them: this is the first point,
then the second, finally the third.'

'You sure?'

'Uh huh, then you give a clear finish.
You can even say, "In conclusion…"'

'Could give the guys each a point.
I could begin and end it?'

'Great! And be certain to
look around the room at your audience.'

'How are you meant to do that
if you have to read from your notes?'
It sounds like I'm getting
conflicting advice here.

'What is it I tell my students?
Speak, don't read. Be purposeful.
Maintain eye contact.'

Mum reaches across me into the fruit bowl
for a lemon.
'How 'bout your visuals?
You planning on using some?'

I nod. That's one thing in order, at least.
'Brenton's doing the PowerPoint presentation,
Tan will supply him with the notes,
and Freddy'll do the graphics.'

'Goodness, I've only just learned that myself,'
Mum admits. 'And that took me a couple of
professional development sessions.'

'What about ending it?'

'Ah, the crucial bit.
Emphasise your main points.'
Mum cuts the lemon in half
squeezes its juice,
points the vegetable knife at me
stabs it in the air.
'But the most important thing of all.
Don't send your audience to sleep!'

Sleep, I think, *who can sleep
in times like these?*

I meet Bailey at the Railway Station

after she'd rung to suggest we meet in town,
that she'd help me look for a dress.
Mum's given me a new store card
and some strange talk about
how she's had a windfall
and some extra money
I should spend on myself.

In Rundle Mall, Bailey skips along.

'Did I tell you about next term?
I'm doing voc prep.
Can start a Cert II in Hairdressing.'

'While you're still at school?'
I look at her closely.
'Is that what you want?'

'Yep, always wanted to,
just didn't have the courage
to tell anyone before.'

'Amazing,' I say. 'I'm in awe.
it's like you're really grown-up.'

'Well, the salon's happy
and're talking about maybe an apprenticeship.'

'Way to go!' I bump her hip.
'I'm proud of you.'

'Okay, TC.'
Bailey is blushing, I can see.

'Let's focus, you dimwit.
We're here for retail therapy!
Let's get the best damned dinner dance dress
you're ever gonna own!'

'Head of the River's only two weeks away.'
I'm admitting my worst fears
but realise with a thrill
I can now talk to Bailey
about rowing from the outside.
She's not on the inside of that
and it makes us sort of free.

'This week's regatta is a repêcharge.'
I see the face she pulls at me, and explain,
'The races where final teams are chosen –
sorta, down to the wire, you know?'

'Gawd, TC, glad it's you
not me.' Bailey drags me
into Diva. 'Let's start
with some glitz,' she says.

April

For assemblies

at Acacia the whole school
packs into Jefferson Hall.
Assemblies aren't every week
and we don't have to join the orchestra
singing 'Advance Australia Fair', though
I'm glad the musicians do okay,
maybe better than the cassette tape at Lighthouse.

Ms Carrick leads the way.

'She's so old, she even taught my dad French,'
Sarah whispers as we file in.
When the noise of seats being folded down subsides,
Carrick stands, positions herself
between two empty chairs.
She's as short as a small Year 8,
but dressed in a pencil-thin black skirt,
today has hair pulled into plaits
pinned across her head.
Despite her powdery face, her look is fierce
enough to scare pants off the bravest
and manages to magnetise the crowd
like a snake charmer with a basket of cobras.

'As you know,' she begins,
'we have a very proud tradition at Acacia.'
Movement rumbles across the rows.
'Our school can boast
a host of notable old scholars.'
She turns to the stage wings and gestures,
'And I'm happy today to welcome back
two outstanding sportspersons.'

A man and woman walk towards her.
She beams at them.
'They're to be congratulated
for their selection to represent our state.'

Out into the middle of the stage
traipse our coaches!
Carrick turns to the hall.
'Excellent students in their Year 12 studies,
only three and four years ago,
and each sports blues as well.
Please welcome Shelley Marshall and Joe Rositano.'

A thousand and fifty-six students
clap like crazy. They clap and clap.
A Year 9 across the aisle whistles.
Chairs are flopped up and down, creating a racket.

'Be quiet, school,' Carrick commands.

I think how if it had been Lighthouse
she would've had no hope of gaining any quiet.
Even here, it's an effort. First, front row students stand up
still clapping, and other rows follow.
It's a Mexican wave.
You just have to stand when your row does.

'Sit down. All of you.'
But it isn't the tone of menace in her voice.
It's Shelley, and Joe, making shushing noises,
motioning for us all to sit down, that does the trick.

That night

Alex simmers as we run a bridge weir.
'Shelley, you didn't warn us
you were coming to school.'

'Or that Joe would be coming,'
says Sarah over her shoulder.
'Or representing the state.'

I say, 'I didn't know you both were so famous!'

'You never mentioned the sports blues,' says Hen.
'What did it feel like, getting one?'

We're halfway round the circuit.
I'm puffed already but Shelley can run
and smile and talk without trouble.
'Well, historically, you can really only
wear a proper blue if you've represented Oxford
or Cambridge in their boat races,' she says.

'You haven't done that!' I'm in awe.

'No, of course not, ninny.
Though I hope to see those regattas
when I go to England next year,' she says.
'Carrick was talking about Acacia's blues,
awards that go to students who excel in any sports.
They're presented at the end of year assembly
when Year 12s get their prizes.'
'And you and Joe won them.'
Sarah sounds impressed. 'Like my brother.'

'Yes, like Dylan,' says Shelley, stopping.
We're at the base of university footbridge.
Glad of the break, I lean against it.

'You know, Sarah. He could give us a hand coaching
if he comes back,' she says.
'When Joe and I go away next year,
the club'll be short. Ask him sometime.'

'Sure. Any chance and I'll give him a call,'
she promises. She looks at us and winks.

We're joined by the senior crews
and Joe starts whistling.

'Hey, coach, that's nice.
What is it?' Hen asks.

'*Water Music*. Composed by Handel
to celebrate a boat race, you know?'

'Yeah, the poncy Poms from their
public schools on the Thames.'
Scarlett and Phoebe fresh from success
in the Melbourne regatta seem drawn to us.

'Not only the well-off rowed,
there were also the watermen,' explains Shelley.

Joe isn't convinced. 'You can't tell me
there wasn't discrimination then.
The wealthy gents versus mechanics et cetera.'

'Sure, not until mid-twentieth century
was there a proper governing body
to regulate the sport.
Now of course it's FISA
that's the international body.'

I'm still a beginner, but figure it's better
to ask and know than be silent and dumb.
'FISA?'

'*Fédération Internationale des Sociétés d'Aviron.*'

'Oh.'

'Whadabout girls rowing?'

'In the Olympics since the fifties.'

'So, how about us, 2020. First eight? Mm?'

'Okay, TC. Whatever you say.'

In the dark of the boatshed

on my way to the ergos,
I hear my name being called.
Hen stands outside, waving.
I come out into the sunshine.
Alex and Sarah face me.

'Repêcharge's this Saturday.'
Alex squares her body at me,
purses her lips.

'We saw the girls from Rutherglen
in Rundle Mall. They laughed at us,'
Sarah says. 'That's not right.'

'Those Rutherglen girls are the limit,'
I say. 'A couple of their friends
wolf whistled me and my friend Bailey.'

'Yeah, well, it's only a couple of them.
But they're real cats,' says Sarah.

I think about how in our school
most of the rowers are supportive.
Only a few aren't duds, like Scarlett and Phoebe,
but they're the minority,
everyone makes allowances for them.
Even when my crew was mean,
they didn't cut me for too long.
We're sticking back together.
Sarah looks straight at me.
'Hen's been in crisis about rowing
since the accident. She thinks
she shouldn't be out there if she can't swim.'

My heart is pierced.
'But she's a wonderful rower
and we need her!'

'Let's get some revenge,' says Alex.

'What we need is an advantage,' says Sarah.
'But I don't know what.'

When Shelley and Joe arrive, we surround them.

'Coaches,' Alex starts.
'You're teaching us really well…'

'But you need to understand
we are prepared…' Sarah chips in.

'To give it one hundred and fifty per cent…'

'We want Rutherglen to get it this weekend.'

'And get it good.' Sarah punches the air
then thumps Shelley and Joe's upper arms
for good measure.

'Let's start tonight at training.'

Joe covers his face with his raised arm,
acting as if to fend us off.
'Okay, okay, already!'

'We'll give it some thought,
truly we will!' Joe scratches his nose,
clearly exasperated.

The coaches disappear into the boat shed
Hen wraps her arms around us.
'Their new boat's so good,' moans Hen.
'But I'm fired up.'

'Our anger can fuel us.'

'Lift our rate!'

'Step it out!'

'As long as we're in this together,'
Hen says, 'and we really zap
training sessions this week!'

Then she has us join hands
before we run in to the ergo machines.

After training

Sarah's dad picks us up.
'Had a pleasant time, girls?'
He juts out his chin
peers through his glasses.

'Sure!' Alex curls her lip.
'It was utter relaxation!'
As we climb into the back seat of his Audi,
she whispers to me and Hen,
'What does he think we do?'

'Sh,' Sarah hisses back.
'He's just jealous.
Wishes he could still do it himself.'

'Do what, darling?'

Sarah jumps. 'Hey, Dad,
I'm gonna start weight training.'

Sarah, like the rest of us,
has been observing the seniors.

Unlike them, we aren't allowed to lift yet.
'Wait till off-season,' Joe had said.
'You can prepare for the spring camp then.'

'Hey, weights, that's fantastic,'
Sarah's dad says.
'I loved yanking all those metal bells
back in the days when I rowed.'

Alex stifles a guffaw.

He turns to Sarah. 'Mm, Sweetie-pie,
don't know why I didn't think of it before.'
He says, unbelievably, 'Maybe
I could buy equipment for home.
We could both use it.'

'Sarah means we can begin weight training
when we finish the summer season, Mr Freeman.'
Hen seems a stickler for the obvious.
'The seniors were giving us some advice,
'bout our approach to training.
They thought our coaches
weren't being hard enough on us.'

Alex hurumphs. 'Endurance, flexibility,
conditioning and strength.
They went on how we'd need it.
I've got that!'
Alex looks us a challenge.

'We all have that. I mean,' she says,
looking at me with a raised eyebrow,
'we're all strong and confident.'
She leans back and looks out the window.

I glance across at Hen.
Her face wears an expression
that says she suddenly isn't so sure.
At the traffic lights
Sarah punches her father's arm.
'Hey, Dad, Dylan can use the weights
when he's on leave, too.
He'd love that.'

'When we see him next,
you ask him, Sweetie-pie. All right?'

'Okay,' says Sarah, uncertain.
'If he makes it home in time for the Head.'

In the quad

the hierarchy is long established.
Stroke position, furthest from the bow, is best rower.
That's Sarah, she's most skilled.
She sets the timing.

The cox guides us with the rate
we have to achieve in order to pull ahead,
make a proper run at the race's course.

In the boat, Hen holds the next position,
then me, then Alex, the strongest rower,
good at last position.

Her bow role useful for levelling our boat,
keeping us from straying
into the paths of other boats.

In newer boats, like Rutherglen's,
coxes sit facing the front of the rig.
Internal sound systems relay their orders
along to the crew.

In our tub, coxes sit facing bow position.
In this case, Alex.

We are poised at the riverbank.
This is our last night's training session
before Saturday's regatta.
Joe crouches on the shore,
his voice low and conspiratorial,

'I think it's time
we tried something new,
something you haven't mastered yet.'

He doesn't smile.
'The racing start.'

Alex crows, 'Yes! At last!'

Sarah explains to a confused-looking Joe,
'It's the secret weapon.
Just what we wanted, coach.'

In the qualifying regatta

starting line in lane three
Rutherglen's A quad girls sit supremely confident,
their matching crimson zoot suits unruffled,
hats perched at the same angle
on their matching heads.

Behind me, Alex growls.

'Remember,' I remind her, 'all for one.'

This is the race for placement
for the big one, the Head itself.
If we're gonna be placed, that is.
This repêchage race determines
whether we'll even race in the finals.

Acacia has more rowing athletes this year
than ever before. We're doing great.
I want to prove to Shelley and Joe
their faith in us newbies is justified.

We're starting with a racing start.
We've practised only once.
But with Hannah coxing,
I'm sure we can manage it.

'Full crew sitting at three-quarters,'
she calls. 'Attention. Row!'

We go, pulling from the three-quarter slide
to half, then back to three-quarter.
Only then do we go into full slide.

Facing backwards like you do in rowing
means at the start you can almost pull the boat
to a stop each time your weight is back,
so with a racing start we can minimise the drag.

It goes without a hitch
and we can all tell the difference.
We're up with the leading crews.
Rutherglen is ahead by half a length
then City Central lunges forward.
They're neck and neck but
we're dropping behind.

'Do ten, as hard as you can,'
Hannah calls in her Lucifer voice.
'Now harder.'

Sarah at stroke is setting our time.
She's rowing like a robot.
In our old boat Hannah faces Sarah.
City Central's Year 10 quads are boats like ours,
but Rutherglen has its new boat.
Their cox sits underneath at the bow end,
calls to her crew through an internal loudspeaker.

I have no time to contemplate the justice
of our different technologies.
We are rowing.
We are in the repêchage,
we are running a solid third.
Then City Central pulls ahead of Rutherglen.

Rutherglen's cox goes crazy
and within a length or two
they've made up the distance.
With City Central's dash ahead
then levelling again with Rutherglen,
they all seem to lose heart.
Before we know it, we're alongside them both.

'Harder,' cries Hannah.
City Central drops away
and we stream just ahead of Rutherglen.

The finishing line is close.
I can hear yelling from the banks
but all I can do is follow the lead of Alex
ahead of me.
Half a length to the finish
and we pull decisively ahead.
We cross the line then sink forward.
Rutherglen cross and, likewise, collapse.
I feel exhausted, too. But I can't believe it.
We've won! Not just come second.
It's great.
Mum and other parents run down at the water's edge,
join us as we row in.
They're clapping, hopping about, whooping like kids.

Shelley jumps and yells and waves her hands.
Then she wades, fully clothed, right into the water.
'You dearest, dearest girls,' she screams,
catching hold of the bow. 'You've got it in you!'

She pauses and catches her breath.
'D'you know what this means?'
She looks at each of us. No one speaks.
'It means you're in with a chance,'
she screams, 'for the Head!'

Joe waves from the beach, not looking happy.

'Hey, coach,' asks Alex when we get near to him.
'Where's the praise?'

'Yeah,' says Sarah. 'We good enough now?'

Joe frowns. 'Bad news, I'm afraid.'
'Just heard from a parent, who heard it on the radio.
Someone discovered it last night.
On the Torrens, there's an algal bloom.
E. coli levels dangerously high.'

'So?' I say, too tired to care.
He wipes a finger across his throat.
'It's kaput, closed, out of bounds.'
We all stare at him.
'No more rowing there,
which means bang
goes our last training session.'

Hen looks round at me, Alex and Sarah,
and bursts into tears.

Dragon boats

bright as jewels, multicoloured as flags,
fly up and down West Lakes.
After a last-minute petition from
Acacia Rowing Club Governing Council,
the Dragon Boat association gave permission
so today we can share their space.
Our boats strange companions on the water
at this, our last training session
only three more nights before the Head
– we're lucky to be here.

A strong wind's whipping up lake water
and I stand watching waves
chop flat smack onto the beach
near the school's trailers
while we wait for a coaches' meeting
of this extraordinary session.
Seniors join juniors,
dragon boats join rowing craft.
Everything is out of order
because the river's closed.

Out west, beyond the dunes, over the sea,
a full-blown storm is lurking.
Clouds are putty purple and
I can feel the hairs on my arms prickling.
Drums are thrumming on the dragon boats,
but the sound is faint,
blown the other direction by the wind.
We should be unpacking our boats
but nobody seems keen to move.

This is our last training, the A team,
Year 10s, chosen for the top quad.
On Saturday we'll be tested to our limit.
We've never trained here before
and it doesn't feel right.

'Wish it was the Torrens,' I say
to no one in particular. 'At least
we'd know the routine. I feel odd being here.'

'Who'd want to be there?' says Hen.
'I'd be too scared to row in that yucky water.
You could get really sick.'

No one mentions our dunking.
She's thinking of it, anyone can tell.

'How come you've got sunglasses on, Sarah?'
Hen asks. 'It's overcast.'
A fierce gust blows.
Sarah's hair lies across her face
so she swipes it behind her ears
only to have it stray immediately.

'Sand.' She points to her eyes.

I rub at my mine, gritty since we arrived.
'As long as it's not like this on the weekend
– tricky to stay on course with such a crosswind.'

Alex turns her back on the water
kicks at the tussocky grass bordering the beach.

Sarah pulls on a cap,
not her usual grey-green and yellow rowing tank,
pulls down the brim to her sunnies.

My skin itches and I want to sneeze.

'You! Dawdlers. Why don't you hurry up?
Someone shoves my back
and it's all I can do not to topple into the water.

I turn to find the senior, Nick,
looking thunderous as the day.

'Hey!' I say. 'Don't do that!'

'Well, don't you go round being so useless,'
he replies, mimicking my voice.

'Aren't you rowing in the first eight?'
Hen asks him, flicking back her hair,
ignoring his bad humour.

'Not unless you lot get moving
and get your boat off the rest of ours.'
He strides back to the trailers.

Pwoof goes any hope I might have had
imagining he'd be boyfriend material.
I allow a brief moment of wistfulness
for the dream-boat Glenelg guy.

'Come on,' says Sarah.
'Let's find our cox and she can help.'

Clouds grow black as bruises

and my arms gooseflesh.
I could've at least have brought a jacket
but am wearing only shorts and singlet.
The quad's standing knee deep in the water
when our coaches return.

'Good work, you guys,' says Joe.

'Don't call us guys,' says Alex.
'It's always bugged me. We're girls.
You should be proud of that.'

'You look organised,' says Shelley,
ever the diplomat. 'That bodes well.'
I think her smile is forced.
'And this weather is good.'

'Huh!' I say. 'This weather's rotten.
The wind's like some frigid banshee,
any time now we're going to be pelted with rain.'

Hen raises one eyebrow, Sarah crosses her arms,
Alex lets out her trademark explosive 'hurumph'.

'You're prepared,
ready for the challenge,' Shelley says.
I don't think we look convinced.
'For the Head, my dearest quad.
This weather's good practice for the Head.'

Then somehow

we manage to turn it all around.
One minute we're disgruntled and reluctant,
next, we're rowing like dragons ourselves.
Perhaps it's Sarah taking off her sunglasses
– fine raindrops have begun to fall –
or Alex, turning her face up to the sky
saying the rain was nice,
but we row hard and we row fast.
We've perfected our racing start,
we'll perfect our racing finish.

Our cox is Claire and she keeps us at it.
Then the rain buckets down and we're drenched.
Rivulets trickle down my singlet to my bra,
trickle through my shorts down to my knickers.
A deluge as brief as it is heavy,
then with the end of the rain
the wind drops.
Suddenly, I can better hear the drumming
from the dragon boats further down the stretch,
regular and strong, in a curious way comforting.
Our quad keeps its line,
doesn't stray in front of other boats.
Over the last two hundred metres
we even lift our rate perfectly in time.

Nick stands alongside Shelley and Joe
at the lake's edge.
'Well done, guys,' says Joe.
'I mean, girls.'

'Are we happy?' asks Shelley.

'Good work,' says Nick
a lopsided smile lighting his face.

Hen bats her lashes, looks up at him –
Alex, Sarah and I notice,
cover our laughter with splutters.

'Well?' demands Nick.

'Well, it's your turn now,' says Hen.
'Let's see how good you are, hey?'

Our Head of the River breakfast

is held naturally at Sarah's house.
Her father's really excited
is even dressed in school colours.
You can tell Sarah's embarrassed.

He shows us pictures of him rowing.
In his study he has a poster-sized print,
him resplendent in a state eight.
Next to it hangs a singlet.

'I hope it's not smelly,'
I whisper to Alex, who laughs.

None of us actually eat much food,
even garbage-guts Hen,
though we should.
I really must have a case of nerves
and have to visit the toilet
before we leave.

On the wall of the family room
another framed singlet.
I take a second look and see the photo next to it.
The boy, my inside-head voice sings,
the pale-skinned, pink-cheeked handsome one.
Also in a state eight picture.

'I see you've found Dylan's singlet,'
says Sarah, coming up behind me.
'I almost didn't want to admit to it
once Dad showed you his.'

'I saw you!' I say. 'Boxing Day at Glenelg.
You and, it must have been, your brother,
were catching a tram.'

'I remember that day,' Sarah says.
'That was just before Dylan went to the AIS.'

'He's at the Australian Institute of Sport?'

'Yep. Dylan dropped out of Year 12
halfway through last year
then got accepted there,
so he's doing Year 13 at Canberra High
as well as rowing.
Spending the year staying with our cousins
in their Belconnen house.
He rides his bike to school and the AIS.
The ACT's a really great place
for riding bikes, you know.'
Then she gives me a sly look.

'I didn't mind him going east.
My cousin's a bit of a hunk,
and with Dylan's staying
I've re-established contact.
Patrick and I Facebook all the time
– you should check it out –
and I think my aunt's gonna invite me over
or else they're gonna come here
for the holidays.'

'Did you say he was coming for the race?'
I feel shaky now as well as queasy.

'Yeah, he's driving across with another family,
don't know when he'll make it in,
but I wish he'd get here soon
to help keep Dad off my back!'

Then, after we've both gone to the loo,
suddenly it's time to go.

We leave to find a car park at West Lakes.
It's difficult, even as early as we arrive.

'There'll be no spaces within the quarter hour,'
Mr Freeman predicts.
We've organised to meet Shelley and Joe
at the palm trees near the playground.
Acacia's setting up its tents nearby.
Volunteer parents run a sausage sizzle
selling soft drinks through the day.

They've tucked away cool bottles of water for us.
Mum put her name down on the roster
and it's weird, but there's a nice-looking guy
looking after Sammy
and their eyes are the same bright blue.

The weather's going to be kind,
warm, but not too warm.
At least the wind is gentle, not breezy.
Nick and other seniors sit in a circle
near the boats at the palm trees
playing cards.

'Wanna join in?'

asks Nick, looking up at Hen.
'There'll be lots of waiting around, you know,
and it'll get pretty boring.'

Hen is knobbly-kneed and cross-legged
beside him in a flash.
With a shrug, Alex and Sarah join them.
But there's so much to see
I keep walking down the length of the course.
How different this Head of the River is
from the last ordinary regatta here.
Parents and friends are pouring in.
All the schools have tents and marquees erected.
Everyone has banners out.
All down the strand, buntings and balloons,
rainbow colours of school teams.
I've never seen Acacia
displayed in so much finery.

Then I'm aware I'm now hollow with hunger,
the lack of breakfast has caught up,
and I go to the grill plate and Mum's there.

'Hey, I'll make you a bacon and egg roll.'
She watches as I gobble it down.
'I've some news for you,' she says.
'I've been meaning to tell you for a while now.
Turn round.' It's the nice man with Sammy.
'Sammy's dad, Pete,' she says.

'Returned from Antarctica. He's the one
whose letter I got – a year late, it turns out.
And the money for your dress,
he wanted you to have it.'

I can't speak. Sammy looks so happy
with Pete holding him,
gazing at my mother,
I feel caught up.

'We're going to be a family,' says Mum.

'Mum!' I say, exasperated. 'We always were!'

Alex hollers from the shore.
'Come on, TC, Shelley and Joe want a word.'

I disentangle myself from Sammy's embrace.
Mum's asking Pete whether he wants breakfast.

'We'll be cheering for you,'
Mum calls as Alex drags me away.

'I'll be cheering, too,' chimes in Pete,
waving Sammy's hand for him.

In the Head of the River

our quad's race is scheduled early.
At least we don't have to begin the regatta
so there's some time to relax into it.
Punters, I'm told, watch Year 10s for their potential,
even though theirs aren't the prime races.
Everyone'll be waiting for Year 12s
first eights, girls' and boys' finals.
Occasionally, over its twenty-year history,
Acacia has won those prestigious races.
Shelley says the girls' eight this year
has real prospects.

Today will be our big chance.

We gather around our trusty tub, the *Jonathon Buck*.

'Strength,' starts Joe.

'Endurance and speed,' we finish for him in unison.

Joe drops his voice.
'Now, I don't need to tell you anything.
Though you haven't been at this sport for very long,
you're pros. All I want you to know is…
I'm proud of you.'

'Hear, hear,' adds Shelley.

'We wanted to tell you what a pleasure it's been
for us coaching you…er, girls.'

'You wonderful darlings,' adds Shelley.
'It's been a great diversion
from writing tedious essays.
And a reminder to us
why we got into this sport in the first place.
Joe and I are better rowers because of you.
Coaching has meant learning more about ourselves.'

'Yeah, and you lot of course!'
Joe grins a showing-teeth grin.

'Now for the race,' says Shelley.
'Let's leave feel-good talk behind
and get down to business!'

'We want you to start strong
and keep up your pace,' Joe instructs us.

'Don't let any other team
put you off your stride,' Shelley adds.

'Actually, all we want to say is,
go get 'em!'

Our boat arrives at the start line

with plenty of time to spare
so we take a breather in our seats
and I remember to breathe deeply.
Time to settle for a bit.

The As quad final will follow the Bs.

While we wait our turn to line up,
our boat hangs at the edge of the field.
It's so hectic, there are more people on land
or boats on water
than I've ever seen
at any regatta ever before.

The pressure's enormous.

It takes us a while to realise,
but there's an official yelling at us.
In all the hustle of our preparation
it's hard to believe
someone's finding fault with us.

I recognise the black Greek-captain's cap first.
It's the same official who was angry with us
months ago at the start of the season.
At our first race he bellowed
and he's doing it again.

'Team Three, you're carrying the incorrect number.'
'No, we're not,' Claire, our cox, says to us.
'I'm sure it's right.'

She calls back to the official.
'No, sir, we are correct.'
'You are not carrying the correct lane number
for the race, Team Three.'

'This is not our race, sir,' Claire calls.

'This is your race, Team Three,
and you are carrying the incorrect number.
Please move to lane five and get set.'

Claire becomes confused.
We're all now confused.
The race is about to start,
and they're waiting,
waiting for us to start.

We line up in lane five.

'Are you ready?' he calls. 'Row!'

Claire sets the rate

Sarah at stroke
starts us hard from the start.
We follow her lead.
We know it's not right
but there's nothing we can do
but row.

'Harder,' screams Claire.
'Give it one hundred per cent!'
Her voice is hoarse even before the halfway mark.
The other teams aren't our usual competitors,
– they're the Bs.
We should be able to beat them easily.
But rowing the wrong race feels wrong.

We lose coordination, and time.
Jerk by jerk, bit by bit, we drop behind
disordered, out of sync.

I'm trying so hard, straining to my limit,
dying with the effort.

This is the same length of race
as ever before
but time has slowed.
It feels twice as long.
It's as if we'll never reach the end.

We near the finish line

and from the shore
cheering reaches through the haze
of pain, of effort.

A small distant thought in my mind,
beyond the agony of the race,
is whether Mum, her new man, or maybe even Dylan
is cheering us on.

Would they recognise us, B final and all?

When it's over, we all flop.
Hen, exhausted to the point of collapse,
cries as if she'll never stop.
Alex, Sarah and I, join in.
It's impossible not to,
and our disappointment is overwhelming.

We watch as the A quad race runs.
Acacia's B team does appallingly –
they can't keep their line
stray off far towards the opposite shore.

Racing officials at the edge
guide them back and they limp in very last.

At the water's edge

coaches and parents run to us.
Joe blows across
like a tempest at full tilt.
He's heard about what happened at the start line
from a parent on a boat.
Both our teams have been disqualified, naturally.

Everyone looks confused.
Seniors and others mill around us.
Nick comforts Hen, at least.

'Rotten luck,' says the Rutherglen A quad stroke.
'We were really sorry not to have you
giving us the good challenge we knew you would.'

'Come with me, crew,' says Joe. 'We'll have a talk.'

Joe's words are good

and Shelley weighs-in too,
and Hen has us join hands
so we cry together until we laugh
– I don't know how that works –
then go watch the rest of Acacia's races.

On shore, the seniors take us under their wings.
Hen, especially, under Nick's wing.
We stand on the rocks near the finish line.
Bailey and Ant even turn up, hand in hand.

'You didn't see me race!' I yell at her, in fun.

'Next year, okay? Promise.'
She's full of plans for moving in with Ant's family.
He says his mum and her partner are pleased
since their place is big enough
for the extra company.

'It'll be good,' says Bailey. 'Mum says I can visit,
maybe babysit Cheri sometimes.'

Fish has tagged along and goggles at me
in my damp rowing singlet.

That's all you'll get, bozo, I think,
and note Scarlett and Phoebe
circling round him, interested.
The Year 11 boys' quad wins
– a first ever for Acacia –
and we all scream ourselves hoarse.

When Nick splashes us all before his race,
we have to stop Ant from starting a fight.

The boys' first eight comes second.
The Year 12 girls' eight win
and we go crazy all over again.

It's a long day
and only when it's drawing to a close
do I see Sarah, with her father,
her brother in tow
him looking at me, taking me in,
me looking at him, taking him in.

And we are introduced.

At the Lakes Hotel that night

for the dinner dance, Joe and Shelley
are actually dancing.
Joe looks goofy, two left feet.
Maybe they're enjoying themselves
more than they imagined they would.

We're having fun at our table.
Mum and Pete are dancing cheek to cheek.
Sammy's asleep in his travel cot
back at the Dysons' place on the Esplanade.

Dylan asks me to dance.

I can't say how it feels.
As if the floor is made of clouds?
That in my dress Bailey helped me choose
I feel like some mermaid who's found her legs,
can dance across the water?
Corny, I know,
but it's like the air
is breathing romance.

When the song ends,
I'm steered back to my seat.

'May I join you?'

Der. 'No, of course not,' I tell Dylan,
and he smiles and sits anyway.

Nick's already there with Hen,
deep in conversation,
Sarah's on the phone to her cousin
– even Alex is animated,
a Year 12 girl advising her on weights training.

I'm almost speechless,
but amazed to find the night disappearing
in dancing, talking, even eating.
Dylan tells me all about Canberra,
how he's making his way.

I don't think about what tomorrow will bring
or if our next rowing trip
could be Lake Burley Griffin.

The quad crew's philosophical
about the day's disastrous muck-up.
Ms Carrick comes over to our table.
'Just giving my condolences, my dears.'
We giggle when she leaves.

Hen shoves in the last of her chocolate mousse.
'Gawd, someone tell me to stop.
I'm stuffed so full.'

'Well, that's it for the season,' Sarah says.

Hen looks surprised.
'I never thought about that.
Of course, we're free.'

'No more training?
You mean I can sleep in again?'
I'm ecstatic. Or am I?

'Only five months to go, though,' Sarah adds,
exchanging looks with her brother.

'Till what?'

'Training camp,' they intone together.

'What? Another one?' Hen can't believe it.
'Don't you mean January, the week before school?'

'No, that's then and the next one's the next one,'
says Nick, laughing at her.
'Next season starts September,
week after the Royal Show.
We go for a long weekend
to the spring training camp.
Get in shape for the season's return.'

'Just when I thought I could take up golf,'
says Alex, reaching over my plate,
lifting the last of my crème caramel.
'Thanks, TC,' she says, grinning.

'And guess what?'
Sarah has a smug look on her face.
'We won't be juniors any more, you know.
And that means something.'

'Yes we will,' I say. 'We'll still be Year 10s.'

Sarah stretches her arms above her head.
'For the purposes of rowing,
we'll be considered one grade higher.'
She closes her eyes.
'That means double the training sessions.'

'Oh,' I say, widening my eyes at Dylan.

He wraps his arm around my shoulder
pulls me close.
'You'll do fine, you pirate queen,' he says.
'You'll endure.'

And we all groan.